WESTERN AVENUE
AND OTHER FICTIONS

Camino del Sol
A Latina and Latino Literary Series

WESTERN AVENUE
AND OTHER FICTIONS

Fred Arroyo

THE UNIVERSITY OF
ARIZONA PRESS

TUCSON

THE UNIVERSITY OF ARIZONA PRESS

www.uapress.arizona.edu

Library of Congress Cataloging-in-Publication Data
Arroyo, Fred, 1966–
Western Avenue and other fictions / Fred Arroyo.
p. cm. — (Camino del sol: a Latina and Latino literary series)
ISBN 978-0-8165-0233-2 (pbk. : acid-free paper)
I. Title.
PS3601.R725W47 2012
813'.6–dc23

                          2011043553

Publication of this book is made possible in part by the proceeds of a permanent
endowment created with the assistance of a Challenge Grant from the National
Endowment for the Humanities, a federal agency.

Manufactured in the United States of America on acid-free, archival-quality paper
and processed chlorine free.

17   16   15   14   13   12   6   5   4   3   2   1

En Memoria de señora Monserrate Pérez Rivera
Nació el 13 de marzo de 1923
Falleció el 8 de febrero de 2011

y para Charles Francis Arroyo
que descubre la vida
en breves gestos

WESTERN AVENUE
AND OTHER FICTIONS

ARRIVAL, CIRCA 1976, EL MORRO

His memory arrives with the geography of this photograph: a
black iron lamppost, a white globe circling above, the blue stone
road, the forking paths and incandescent fountains, a labyrinth
of arcades leading from the bright heart of the city to its darker
edges, *el Morro*, that blackish sea-sprayed wall, sentry of depar-
tures and arrivals, timekeeper of the azure sea. Palm trees sway
in the breeze. The sweet smell of the rum distillery wafts across
the bay tinged with smoke, the sweaty shapes of oxen struggling in a cane field, the fragrance of purple orchids beginning to
bloom on the edge of a cascading waterfall bathed in the moun-
tain green of dusk. Crouched down, against the lamppost, he's
dressed in a yellow and red striped T-shirt, khaki shorts, and a
pair of delicate-looking leather sandals. Beside him, almost sol-
emn with newness, a valise the color of deeply bruised fruit. His
father approaches, he turns, hears it is time to go, clutches the
valise, lets go, crouches even more, his butt barely touching the
cool blue stones as he follows the designs of facades and porticos,
Santa Barbara's church bell swinging with bass and echo within
the arcades, the road, out toward the wall of el Morro and back
again, like a sudden spark or surge, and he's standing. He turns.
Inside the Park of Pigeons, men sit on wooden beer crates underneath the last tiger-striping shade of the trees, their dominoes
cracking, the sun slowly descending like a peeled orange ripe
with heat, their laughter. His father lifts the valise, the pigeons
springing up into the bluing evening light, suddenly alabaster as
if written in perfection by a strange hand, perhaps spoken into
form by a foreign tongue just on the edge of the palms shaking
for the comings and goings of the sea.

A CASE OF CONSOLATION

Boogaloo lived in a small quarter of the city, an indistinct district bordered by certain streets he never liked to cross, and where no one asked his name. Boogaloo—born Manuel Perez—lived in an old brownstone on the top floor, almost level with the El, where in the spring he watched for the tops of the trees suddenly to bud green, the bowl of sky above Chicago slowly bluing with a vast space that mirrored his anonymity. The high beige walls of his room held no pictures, and the clean and shiny wood floors caused the room to shimmer on bright sunny days like an undiscovered sea. He sometimes sat on a folding chair in the sunlight, strips of light falling through the blinds, and when the train rumbled overhead passing by, he leaned back a little and turned his head, as if listening to something very important.

Braced on the wall was a single bookshelf, and on the shelf he had placed a few seashells, a copy of M.F.K. Fisher's *Letters*, the well-traveled *Comida Criollas*, a cracked, leather-bound volume from the late eighteenth century on new Hispanio vegetation and foodstuffs, *Fruiticas Paradisio*, Nietzsche's *Human, All Too Human*, and the three volumes that make up Seneca's *Moral Essays*. In these essays some passages were starred, a few sentences underlined. A particular passage had exclamations along its edges, which Boogaloo had copied by hand in blue ink on a three-by-five card; with a few small pieces of tape, he had placed it in the middle of the wall next to his shelf. He would reread the passage often when his room filled with the incomprehensible weight of shadows.

In the corner of the room, on the edge of the shelf and below the passage, Boogaloo had a small folding table of wood. On the table were sheets of butcher paper he had cut as close as possible to ten by ten, a white paper cup from a coffee shop holding black and red wax pencils and a few number two cedar pencils, some gold clips and an orange barrel-shaped sharpener on a shallow, clear dish, and a stack of three-by-five cards next to the cup.

In the center of the table there was a recent recipe he had composed, the wax cursive script working through intricacies of the mangoes and smoked Spanish pepper, a rice dish Boogaloo was striving to master. There were several sheets with drawings of a simple, ideal kitchen he dreamed of working in, the majority of the space dominated by a thick butcher-block table (he could see how in the future it would be oily and rich with colors—saffron, oregano, cilantro, garlic, and olive oil—that became a part of the wood's nature), a six-burner stove with a flat grill, and a small stone oven. He drew a small alcove in one of the kitchen's walls, where he sketched in a chair and a desk with a small goose-necked lamp. He set his pencil down. He listened to the robins chirping outside his window. He picked up his pencil and wrote *10* and *15* on a card, then totaled them. Direction: Soak rice in 1/4 cup of coconut milk for *30* minutes before cooking.

He had not taken a drink in ten years and had not seen his daughter in over fifteen.

Most of Boogaloo's life was held, during the somewhat good times, in a suitcase, and, during the not-so-good times, in a paper bag. He moved from job to job, although work was always defined for him not by the specific task but by the places he experienced: a kitchen dishroom in a squat, steam-shrouded basement where his eyelashes collected little silver flecks of water and soap bubbles; the long and thin red rows of dirt between tobacco plants, his shoes caked with dirt, and his socks never seeming to lose the red ring of dust just below his ankle; the deep and endless blue sky over a beet field; the low and dim light of his helmet, his hands black with manure and dirt in a mushroom cannery; and the brief space—a bubble of musical time shaped by the rhythm of a knife—between a cutting board, prep table, and stove. New York, Connecticut, Michigan, Indiana, Illinois—the slow movement of sweat coursing down the back of his scalp, his sore neck and shoulders, the dull, constant ache in his lower back, and always in need of a new pair of shoes as he found himself moving west. Without ever understanding the gradual changes to his emotional life, Boogaloo was slowly transformed into a man without likes or dislikes, without a strong sense of desire or remorse, a shell alone on an empty beach without the inner, passionate song of the sea found in that place where shell, ear, and sea meet in the radiance of music. Continually in motion—adrift in work—he seemed to simply stand still.

The dream of his kitchen, the quiet new kind of work of his recipes, filled him with a sensation he couldn't quite name, and yet he described the sensation—one sleepless night he saw it on the edges of the shadows that slowly moved across his apartment's walls—in the memory of a childhood hurricane, that quiet moment just before the fury of the storm, when the golden sky looked streaked with guava paste, the sea dark green and thick with deeper currents, and Boogaloo mesmerized by a palm tree swaying in the breeze, its fronds shivering like a horse's mane, his feet solid and heavy in the sand.

Boogaloo's days were spent working in a restaurant on North Clark Street. A very small place, Cassava, with only five tables, most of the business to-go, and the customers either ordering at a small counter separating the dining room and the kitchen or sitting at one of the formica tables. Cassava was one of three in the city, specializing in a fusion of Caribbean and Mexican food made up fast and hot. The top two sellers were a *ropa vieja* burrito and a cubano sandwich. Boogaloo cooked and managed a staff of two: a young Peruvian man, Tomás, who kept the kitchen and dishes clean and helped with the preparation of vegetables and seasonings; and an older Nicaraguan woman, Rosita, who took orders in the dining room and at the register. After work, Boogaloo lost all sense of time as he sat at his table and began the draft of a new recipe. He strove to capture the various smells, flavors, and colors evoked by an established recipe in a book, and then revised as his memory came alive: how his mother had simmered a *soncocho* of chickpeas, pig's feet, habaneros, and cilantro in the afternoon; in the last thirty minutes it took for her white rice to cook, she dropped slices of mango into the soncocho, thickening its consistency and flavor, the habaneros still evident as they painted a thin, strong line of heat along the tongue. Once a recipe was drafted on a piece of butcher paper, he took it the next day to Cassava and tried it out; it became the meal he, Tomás, and Rosita ate in the afternoon lull between 3:30 and 4:30. As they took bites he watched their expressions, tried to note how Tomás licked his lips, casually focused on how Rosita's eyes glazed with the strong sensation of flavor. Boogaloo let the recipe exist in his mind for a time, sat down with a three-by-five card, and in the presence of Rosita's green-blue eyes composed the recipe in a steady hand, his version of the recipe now translated into English.

Boogaloo had no friend or lover in this city. When he left Connecticut with a handful of men to work and live in Michigan, he never imagined how quickly their brotherhood would fall apart, his companions lost to death, marriage, family, and the madness of drink and wandering. Common fates, he thought, yet he couldn't seem to inhabit any of them—save his years of drink—with any passion. He had once had a great love in Michigan. He remembered her shyly undressing on the edge of a sand dune, her breasts dark purple plums in the night, and how the cold wind of the freshwater sea ran along his spine, his eyes almost watering with desire for Ramóna. He listened to the waves crashing against the pier, then hushing on the sand, and his ears filled with the sea of his heart. That was many years ago, yet he still could evoke the smell of the cold air, the grit of sand in between his fingers and trapped in his underwear, in an instant. And their daughter, Magdalene? She became entangled in their longing that night, even though she was not even an idea or a hope then. Now twenty-five years old, now making her way into a world he did not know. His loneliness, his exilic fortune, was the grand meal of his life no one could take away, and it was Boogaloo's fate to chew it—macerate it—every day.

His desire for Ramóna he never felt again. Sometimes, on windy, nighthawk fall evenings, the air wet from the sea, he walked along the shore in his shirtsleeves, his flesh rising to meet the wind and the memory of what was. Magdalene never learned that Boogaloo was her father, and if there were times when he walked along the shore and wept, it was never just for himself.

One evening, a clear blue night in late April, the air smelling clean and tinted with the lilacs Boogaloo had stopped to savor in Lincoln Park that afternoon, thoughts like these shadowed his footsteps down Clark Street. He had decided to stop at Café Intelligentsia for a *cortado*, a few note cards in his shirt pocket to help him mull over the possibilities of yuca and curry. As he turned toward the door, Rosita walked out with a coffee. They greeted each other with surprise, exchanged pleasantries, and remarked about the change of weather, the beginning of spring. Outside the café they sat on a bench, their coffees between them, and continued to talk, sometimes their words lost as a car passed by. That first meeting lasted until midnight, and then two or three times a week they would meet for coffee and conversation once Cassava was closed, Rosita leaving work first and finding them a table in the corner of the café, or if it was too warm inside, at a bench or table out on the sidewalk. Once Boogaloo and Tomás had cleaned up the kitchen, the floor wet and shiny, they stepped into the alleyway. Boogaloo locked the door, and

with their good-byes there was always the *see you tomorrow.*
Boogaloo picked up his step to meet Rosita.

Slowly, over time, Rosita's conversations and presence broke
though his loneliness, as if a blue eggshell surrounding his existence had cracked. Boogaloo became aware of her slender neck,
the thin streaks that highlighted her hair gold and red in certain
slants of light, how she smiled with wistful pleasure after the
first hot sip of coffee. The way her green-blue eyes ravished his
face into a smile. Rosita gradually shared with Boogaloo her life
in Nicaragua. Back home she had a ten-year-old son, Roberto, and
an eight-year-old daughter, Margarita, who were living with her
parents. Her husband, who had worked as a mechanic near the
city center, died during an earthquake, his body discovered under
the collapsed garage. She worked at Cassava and as a seamstress
six mornings a week in a T-shirt factory on the North Side. She
sent as much money home as she could, and hoped to save a little
to bring her children north.

He could never find the right moment to reveal himself,
until one day the eggshell shattered to pieces: a few tables over, a
young boy and his father shared a single steaming cup of chocolate, and from a plate stacked with Scotch shortbread cookies,
they would each take one, lean closer, dip the cookie into the cup,
hold it for a moment, and then raise the soft, wet cookies to their
mouths.

Rosita, my name is Manuel, Manuel Perez.

She had followed his eyes to the other table. She smiled.

Please, call me Manuel.

Boogaloo and Rosita met for coffee often, through the year.
One winter evening they met at the Grant Park Pavilion and
watched a strange movie about the Arctic, windswept regions
scratchy with the shifting and buckling ice, an almost tender
violin in the background. They were both freezing, their breath
clouding in front of them, and they laughed with great joy at
how strange and beautiful it was to sit there in December watching the film of what seemed an even colder place. They left the
pavilion and made their way down Michigan Avenue. The dusk
began to rise all around them, in grays and deep blues, as they
strolled down the avenue, window-shopping in the blaze of
Christmas lights. Little by little Boogaloo revealed the details of
his life, memories of a childhood always close to the sea, how he
never imagined making a living as a cook, and yet, given his vivid
memories of his *abuela* cooking, it seemed natural, even though
he had no sense of where it might lead, what was next.

They were separating to make their way home, Rosita taking the El north, Boogaloo walking the last mile along the edge of Lincoln Park to his apartment. They stood under the tracks, a train thundering overhead. His hands shook at his sides, and he had this feeling he did not want the night to end just yet, even though he had been alone for so long he didn't know how to make it last, and in this state the sudden weight of fright lay heavy on his shoulders. Rosita smiled, clasped his arm, just below his elbow.

Don't go, just yet, she said.

He looked at the ground, shifted his weight to his left foot, wiggled the right in the air, and then stomped it in the cold. Their breath turned silver between them, ghostly butterflies rising, and then disappearing. He nodded.

I have something for you, Rosita said, and then pulled a long red box from her bag. She handed it to him.

Feliz Navidad, Manuel.

He looked at her without expression—perhaps quizzical, a kind of misunderstanding, hesitancy. She held the box between them and then tapped his chest lightly.

For you, for all your friendship.

Boogaloo held the box in his left hand, and then with his right gently shook the lid off. Inside, folded in a neat square, was a scarf elegantly patterned with shades of purple, the fabric a soft silk, the pattern feeling rich against his knuckles. Rosita lifted it from the box, and they both looked quickly as the tissue paper lining the box jumped with the wind and flew down the street, the scarf caught there and unfurling like a flag. She flattened the scarf against her thigh, and then raised it behind Boogaloo's head. She tied it in a loose knot around his neck, tucking the ends of the scarf into the small V of his black overcoat. She flipped the collar of his coat up and smoothed the scarf down on his chest.

Thank you, Rosita. It is too much—the money, your children . . .

She raised two fingers to Boogaloo's lips, lightly touched them, shooshed him quiet. No worries, she said. *Elegante y suave* for you.

He began to loosen the knot.

No, you have all the work you do—and I . . . She grabbed his hands, held them tightly.

Don't. Don't, please don't tell me what I can and can't do. I think of them every day, am so alone here, but you have become my friend in ways I might never be able to speak.

Tears formed in her eyes, green, blue, then silver in the cold. No, it is for you, Manuel.

His lips burned from her touch, and as she started to shiver, he had a great desire to hold her close, for Rosita to feel the heat rising into a bloom on the place where the scarf touched his neck. But his feet felt like concrete, and he couldn't overtake the brief space that separated them.

Thank you, was all he could say.

I'm going to go now, she said, I'll see you tomorrow. She turned, took the first two steps toward the platform. She stopped, turned around, waved.

Unless you want to ride with me?

He closed his eyes for a moment. In the distance, train wheels ground against steel, a horn honked, and a roar of wind filled him with the smell of cooking chocolate from the candy factory on the river. He pressed his hands against his chest, felt for a moment the purple rising in his fingers. Before words arose in his throat, as the wind seemed to die, he heard Rosita say, No worries, Manuel, we'll ride together another day. Her eyes were of the saddest shapes—like split, sea-battered almonds—he had ever seen on her face. He wanted to apologize.

Okay, Rosita. Thank you, I'll see you tomorrow, were the only words he could utter.

Alone again, filled with the loss that followed his indecision. He smiled, and waved. He turned and walked from underneath the El to meet his street.

On his walk home the cold did not bother him, as if he were filled with some great fire. He made a decision: when they met in the evenings, he would wear the scarf with pride, and as they walked down the street, or sat at a table in the café, he would keep his hand close to her side, there on the table crossing over the line that separated them. He would collaborate with accident, hand brushing hand, and in that moment she would know his apology, his desire. He would make an effort to remind Rosita to save her money and bring her children to Chicago—only as a friend, however, and never at the risk of telling her what to do. He stopped in a crosswalk, the streets seemingly deserted, and caught sight of the moon, a blue face looking down between two skyscrapers with delight at his decision. He continued to walk and imagined his upcoming meeting with the owner of Cassava, an East Asian who always took Boogaloo's new recipes to his other locations, and who seemed to trust Boogaloo's judgment. Boogaloo would tell him that in the new year he did not need a raise, but Tomás and Rosita needed one for sure. He could not run the restaurant without them; they kept Cassava spotless, and customers felt they were eating food from good people. They deserved a great amount of credit for that.

When Rosita did not show up for work the next day, Boogaloo felt a rush of worry, for she had never missed a minute of work before. He thought that perhaps he had been too pushy. She had lived all those years without her husband, worked hard with the conviction she must provide for her children. What gave him the right—*carajo*—to tell her anything? Perhaps she was angry, didn't understand why he couldn't simply accept her gift, and didn't want to see him today. Tomorrow, tomorrow, she will return, he said under his breath, grating the pieces of ginger on his cutting board. She will return tomorrow, and you will apologize.

That night Boogaloo's sleep was restless, the wind off the lake rattling his window, and in each moment when he felt himself falling into the dark hole of sleep, he heard grains of sand striking the pane, saw a dune where Rosita stood naked, her hair rising in the wind, the purple scarf wrapped around her neck, her arms wide open, and then himself trying to run, stumbling in the sand, falling just before he reached her.

The next morning he arrived earlier than usual and set to work lacing a pork shoulder with cumin, garlic, and olive oil. He placed it in the oven, and then after the long task of chopping a ten-pound bag of onions for a new batch of salsa, he realized he was sweating. He and Tomás looked up to the sudden tapping at the front door—11:35. Thirty-five minutes past their daily opening.

After you open the front door, Tomás, please put on a clean apron. Do you think you can run the register and wait tables today?

Tomás nodded, set down his knife, wiped his hands on his red-splattered apron, a pile of cubed tomatoes next to his knife. He moved toward the door. Boogaloo felt something was wrong, the deep pocket of his stomach awash with shame—he didn't know for what—as he replayed in his mind that last day with Rosita. It must be because of some anger, some hurt, that she has not returned, he thought. He saw himself in his room, the El rattling overhead outside his window, as he looked into a delicate glass box he held in the palm of his hand, the glass flecked with bright pieces of papier-mâché, and in the bottom of the box a mirror capturing his face. He had bought the box for Magdalene.

He wanted to see her one day and give her the box, so she might forget all the years she did not know him; in that one instant, she could see how beautiful her face had become, how she could live with that face and with more than her memory. Rosita was hurt, yes, perhaps embarrassed, because on the night she gave him the scarf he couldn't let it wrap them together, and when he didn't speak she saw her own mirror: a reflection of exile and loneliness she couldn't bear.

He looked at the clock again, felt his heart jump a beat, and then the blood seeping from his thumb the moment he sliced the edge off. *Shit,* he yelled, grabbing a towel and wrapping it around his pulsing thumb. In one slice of time she had offered him an emotional life he had not felt in years. A train had stopped, a door had opened, and he couldn't step across the threshold to where she stood waiting. Tomorrow, tomorrow, I will apologize, look for the slight opening, the thin slice where I can walk through, Rosita, where skin and blood exist on the other side of a wound.

Two days later Rosita had still not returned. Thinking then, with almost a sense of glee, that she was sick and not angry, Boogaloo called Rosita only to discover that her number was for a shoe store on Armitage Avenue. He called the number once more. The Shoe Palace again.

A week later Boogaloo took the El up to Bucktown, the whole swaying ride his stomach sinking with the feeling that the address on Rosita's application did not exist. The sun was warm pouring through the train windows, sunlight glinting brightly off the tracks, on tin roofs, and at each stop the quickly melting snow from a station's awning dripped like rain in the open door. Down on the street Boogaloo passed a Starbucks, a women's boutique, and then turned the corner and made his way down a block filled with discount furniture and vintage clothing stores. He unzipped the windbreaker he had chosen that morning, the afternoon beginning to turn hot, a warm spell arriving in late January. He loosened his scarf. Scraps of paper scraped in the wind along the sidewalk; he heard a can clank in the gutter.

N. 1885 was a large vacant lot surrounded by a chain-link fence, the lot chock-full of dead grass and weeds, a high pile of dirt in the middle littered with broken pieces of concrete and asphalt, jagged strips of black- and-silver shingles, a confetti of colored bottles, and what looked like a car fender partially buried under the debris. There was a small circle of gritty gray melting snow around the pile of dirt.

Boogaloo stood with his fingers in the fence. He remembered Rosita bent over a table, her hand moving a warm cloth slowly over the top, a red tray of dirty plates and glasses balanced in the other. Her jeans dark and new, tight and smooth, and how her white-and-blue suede sneakers were always brushed and clean. He had touched her only once—really by accident, or perhaps on impulse. Thick wet snowflakes had fallen for a few minutes as they walked down Michigan Avenue, Rosita's hands bundled in mittens as she stood on a corner, trying to move her hair away from her eyes. She was telling Boogaloo how she sometimes hated herself for liking the life of these streets, when back home her family lived on an almost empty red dirt road. He never wore gloves, his dark hands dry and cracked from the cold wind, and as she spoke he raised his hand and tucked her hair back along her ear, and then smudged away a snowflake that had landed just above her eye. They stared at each other, the world seeming to fall away, and they both laughed as the light changed and a surge of people pushed them out into the crosswalk.

A mangy brown dog squeezed beneath the fence, circled the pile of debris with its nose slung low and its eyes on Boogaloo. After circling once, it stopped and stared at Boogaloo, raised its right leg, and then let out a long stream of pee on a green bottle, the deep yellow liquid running down and staining the snow.

He looked at the number again, written in red on a three-by-five card. He tore the card into pieces and then slowly pushed them through the fence, let them scatter on the ground. Rosita had disappeared. Quickly she had entered his life, and now she was just as quickly gone.

Four months passed. Tomás had a cousin, Javíer, who came to work at Cassava. He was young, handsome, with a bright smile and a strong command of English. The customers liked him waiting on tables and ringing up orders; Boogaloo would look out and see them smiling and laughing with Javíer, their menus open as they pointed at dishes, asked questions. Boogaloo still had his recipes, his Sunday walks in the park or along the lake. Possessions never became a necessity—what fit in a paper bag or suitcase was all he ever needed.

Or so he thought. All that winter he had contemplated throwing Rosita's scarf away, yet each time he stood in front of a dumpster, felt the wind tugging it away, his fingers found the fine silk and caressed it with delicacy until his hand warmed with purple, and then he tightened the scarf with force. Now, in May, it was folded and wrapped in butcher paper, up on the top shelf of his closet, awaiting the first cold winds of fall. The presence of purple filling his broken shell—that was all that had changed.

Sitting at Café Intelligentsia one Sunday afternoon, he looked up from the newspaper, rubbed his eyes with his fisted hands, and then struck his forehead with his palms several times, a loud smacking sound rising in the air. A few people turned. He took a drink of his coffee, now cooled and somewhat bitter, little bits of the grounds trapped in the side of his mouth. He gagged, felt a great wave of nausea, and dug the grounds out with his tongue. The espresso machine hissed. A couple at a table in the corner laughed, then leaned in close, kissed. His knees shook with a knowledge he couldn't quite comprehend, and although he had been frequenting this café for the last three years, it was the first time the conversation around him broke through the veil of his isolated existence, as if every conversation he had not noticed before now drenched him. He covered his ears, his knees shaking even more. The words in the Spanish weekly swam before his eyes. He held his legs still, focused hard, and read these paragraphs again:

ICE STEPS UP INITIATIVE

A US Immigration and Customs Enforcement superior, speaking with anonymity because of impending court cases that must not be compromised, discussed the current administration's recent arrests at meat packing plants along the Iowa–Minnesota border. "These operations are in line with an established initiative to address the alarming number of illegal aliens flooding certain parts of the country," the superior said.

"Individuals," he continued, "who are breaking the law, and who are also victims of employers who knowingly break the law."

When this reporter questioned the superior about the parameters of the "established" raids, the superior wanted to correct the misuse of the term "raid," since "these are initiatives to arrest, detain, and prosecute individuals who are breaking the law." He added that this is an initiative in progress, and that beyond the media's focus on the Iowa–Minnesota events, "we have been engaged for some time now in smaller, less visible enforcement in Missouri, Georgia, and even in the larger urban areas of Seattle and Chicago. There are many industries—from meat production to agriculture to apparel—employing people living illegally in the US."

When the superior was questioned about why arrested individuals are moved outside the region of their initial arrest, and why families have been separated, often to undisclosed areas, the ICE superior said, "It is a most painful case when families are separated. Of course, we sympathize, and yet our charge is to best serve the established laws." The superior expressed his regret for this separation, and hoped family members would receive consolation in the fact that the ICE treats every detainee "fairly."

In the end, however, the superior stated that it is "imperative for legally residing relations to think very hard about encouraging or supporting individuals who enter the US illegally."

Various sources suggest that in the past six months between 5,000 and 25,000 individuals have been arrested by the ICE, and there may be as many as 2,000 children affected.

Boogaloo looked up from the paper. The voices in the café now spoke in a quiet din. The young woman from behind the counter approached his table and asked if he was done, and if his coffee was good. Yes, very much so, he said, handing her the cup on the saucer, the small silver spoon on the side rattling with his shaking hand. Thank you, he said; and, Yes, he was done with the paper. He rose and made his way outside.

The tables were crowded, spoons and cups and saucers clinking together, laughter, and too much bare skin for Boogaloo as everyone bathed in the late afternoon sun. At one table a young man had a cantaloupe on top of a *Tribune*, surely his wife sitting across from him, and the boy with long sandy brown hair and the girl with light blue ribbons in her curly black hair his children. He stabbed into the cantaloupe with a Swiss Army knife, followed the line of fruit around its skin, and when the two halves opened, his children clapped, the newspaper becoming wet and dark, the print disappearing in the presence of juice and seeds and shredded pieces of flesh.

Boogaloo headed south, where he would turn east toward the freshwater sea.

At one of the last café tables was a young woman wearing a sheer, peach-colored dress, and on the table in front of her, next to her glistening, tall glass of iced tea, lay a mortarboard. She pulled away the lemon-yellow scarf from around her neck, letting it fall on the mortarboard. May, graduations, and Boogaloo continued on, thinking of how that young woman would leave the older couple sitting with her, how she would thank her parents for everything, her emotional life chaotic with nostalgia and fear, and then a new opening of joy would appear as she realized she had the whole world in front of her, and when looking at a map she would imagine a shifting mass of possibilities moving across and within the colored borders, and she would feel great power in placing her finger in that one region she would learn to control. Magdalene was maybe somewhere in a region like that. Changó, an old friend from Michigan, had told Boogaloo that Magdalene was graduating with a master's degree in education. He wanted to smile but winced at the thought. She had been alone, far away, adrift in her own recipe of memory and desire: living for many years in Ann Arbor, a town he knew nothing of.

A long red dirt road where two children played with an empty can, and Boogaloo tried to see the bend in the road where Rosita appeared and walked home.

Two Latinos passed him on the sidewalk, one raising his chin in hello, both probably on their way to work, given the white shirts and black ties they carried in clear laundry bags.

The sidewalk seemed like a slice of the world he would learn to accept, a form of consolation no one could ever take away: one step in front of the other, one step in front of the other. Ann Arbor. A tree with its branches high and broad and filled with thick purple blossoms, the fragrance of the split cantaloupe, Boogaloo imagining slices of mango sprinkled with smoked Spanish paprika and wrapped in thin slices of Serrano jamón on the menu tomorrow. Perhaps on the plate a small pool of olive oil and three or four almonds. Something *suave, elegante, rich.*

Boogaloo turned east, one foot in front of the other, and he saw within the trees arching over the avenue infinite doorways opening and closing, some with and some without promise. He took each threshold encountered with surprise and wonder, crossing over without any sense of right or wrong. Tomorrow, Rosita, tomorrow if it's warm like today, I will slice fruit, wherever you are, wherever we won't meet, Rosita, tomorrow, please don't be alone.

WAVES

My memories often go out and return like those waves, continuously circling around an island of images: my father standing in the yard with a bottle of beer or rum in his black, grease-stained hand, his tools glinting on a car's fender. Asleep on the couch in the late afternoon without a shirt, missing a shoe, his head cradled in his arm, his hand open and long, almost touching the floor. The sudden rage that reddened his face, and then the angry pitch of his voice as he fell against a doorjamb or knocked over a chair. He often seemed filled with some deep pain he couldn't quite come to terms with. His quietness I remember as much as his drinking; how he would slide underneath a car with a few tools and a lamp and spend hours without a word; how he bent into a beautiful silent arc as he moved his hands deep into thick green leaves and picked peppers or beans; how he sat on an old kitchen chair under a tree, watching puffy, lonely clouds drifting by, a tall glass of ice water glistening next to a neatly folded newspaper.

SOMEDAY YOU'LL SEE

I thought of the block as an art project because of the sailboat carved along one edge, a guitar along the other, and how the lines of each image were filled with black ink or paint. It must have been an art project, perhaps from when Lorime was in the first or second grade. A small four-by-six block of wood. No more than an inch thick. Sanded very smooth and varnished a dark mahogany color. What puzzled me was the photograph shellacked to the block: Lorime smiling, his two front teeth biting his bottom lip gently, his hair curly and even darker in the black-and-white photo, his cheeks marked by dimples, his eyes deep pools of wonder. He was hugging a thick tree, his arms not quite long enough to reach around. He was so young then, six or seven, and I had never seen the photograph. He was wearing an olive-brown safari coat, and I remembered how I had found it at a thrift store, and when I gave it to Lorime he seemed never to take it off. Just before the sixth grade I noticed how the cuffs rose halfway up his forearm, and two buttons were missing from the front. I finally said something about the cuffs, and the next day when he left the house for school, Lorime walked down the sidewalk without the coat.

The other day, out of the blue (that's what people here in Niles, Michigan, say), Begé, my oldest, came home with a manila envelope holding the art project, one green glove, and two pencils. She said her teacher had found them in an old shoebox in a closet with Lorime's name written on the side. She looked at me, her face filled with sadness, her head turned to the side in a kind of question, Mama, *who* was saving these things? I took the block from her, opened my arms, and held her for a moment, humming *Bésame mucho* until she laughed, let go, and skipped from the room. Lorime still there with me—in the grains of wood warm in my hands.

A quarter past four, and not a customer in the bodega. I slipped Lorime's art project back into my apron pocket, grabbed a broom and began sweeping behind the counter, along the edges of the shelves, and then the half circle in front of the entrance that gave way to the bodega's two shiny aisles. The sun fell brightly through the storefront window, the dust rising from my sweeping speckled with flecks of purple, and I hoped that when I picked up my girls they weren't running around outside the library, their coats on the ground. I made a few extra swipes under the bread rack. Bending over, I held the dustpan with one hand and swept with the other, balls of dust and receipts gathering in the pan's mouth. I straightened, walked behind the counter, and dumped the sweepings into the trash can underneath the register. The bell above the door jingled. Mrs. Sanchez walked in, followed by the brief sound of some car racing down the street.

Hola, Maria.

Good day, Mrs. Sanchez.

How's business? she asked.

Real busy around lunchtime, and then not a soul for the rest of the afternoon, I said, untying my apron and slipping it over my head. Ever since the raid, it seems like the street's empty, I said, gesturing outside the window.

Mrs. Sanchez nodded, looked down the aisle at the meat counter; Ramon waved, a knife in his hand, the cuffs of his white jacket stained by bits of meat and blood.

See you tomorrow, then, at eleven o'clock?

Yes, Mrs. Sanchez, I'll see you then. I snapped the dustpan onto the end of the broom and hung it from the small hook on the high shelves behind the counter. She squeezed my shoulder as she passed, and as our eyes met I turned my head down, carefully folding my apron into a bundle, while slipping Lorime's project out of the pocket. I grabbed my purse, folded my coat over my arm, and slid the block of wood into my coat. Tomorrow, I said and waved, and Mrs. Sanchez, looking through some invoices, raised her head, smiled, and waved.

A few years ago Mrs. Sanchez had to take over her husband's little bodega after he died. There was a small meat counter, and two main aisles—one with beans and rice, spices, coffee, and a handful of fresh onions, avocados, bananas, tomatoes, cilantro, and a few kinds of peppers; and another aisle with canned goods, juices, and boxes of cereal. Behind the register, up on the higher shelves, is where all the candy, soaps and detergents, toilet paper and paper towels, shampoo, and a few bottles of rose water were lined. There was a small upright cooler with gallons of milk, cheese, and sodas of pina, coco, and guava. Just the basics, the staples, and yet with the exact kinds of items the small community of Mexicans and Puerto Ricans in this town wanted. Without Alberto at home anymore, with no money coming in, I was grateful for the job, five days a week from eleven o'clock to four thirty. I ran the register, stocked the shelves, and swept the front of the store. Mrs. Sanchez worked early in the morning and then in the evening, and told me she was happy to have the middle of the day off, and just as happy that she could leave the bodega in what she called strong hands.

I went down the small alleyway along the bodega, and when I turned down the next street I could see the top of the library's roof. The sun warmed my back; the trees lining the sidewalk shook in the light breeze, their red bright leaves crinkling together. I stopped. I didn't hear or see the girls. Every day since I began working at the bodega, the girls were first to eat their small snack of crackers and cheese on the way to the library from school, and then they were to spend the next few hours quietly, trying not to draw attention to themselves, just reading or listening to music through headphones, as if they belonged. I could work and know they were safe in the library. Even though fall was in the air, the morning cold with dew and the edges of frost, the smell of apples drifting over the valley, each evening losing a slice of the sun, I often found the girls outside, playing hopscotch or tag, holding sprint races, or playing invented games with leaves and sticks. I stopped again, in case the girls suddenly ran from around the edge of the library. I slipped my coat on, though I was warm, and left the buttons undone. I felt for Lorime's art project—firm, solid—in my coat pocket.

Now, with the meatpacking plant raided, so many workers taken away and families split apart, everyone who came into the bodega spoke of the quiet. The town was silent; its streets still but for the falling leaves. I had already lost too much; I couldn't lose my job. Yellow, green, maroon—I had to gather those falling leaves, those brilliant colors.

I stepped close to the picture window on the side of the library and spotted the girls in the reading room. Begé sat in a high-backed club chair, her feet on an ottoman, a book open on her lap. Marita sat next to her on the chair's arm, one hand resting on Begé's shoulder, the other twisting the ends of her hair. Begé turned the page, then pointed and underlined something. She moved her finger several times on the page, looked at Marita, her eyes wide and clear, her lips turning into a smile. I stepped closer, the sunlight fading back as the shade from the overhanging roof and the light from inside—bouncing off the thick green plants, the neatly lined bookshelves, the tightly woven and patterned carpet of orange and brown squares—filled my eyes.

For a moment, all I could concentrate on were the leaves scraping together on the trees, that wispy sound above me suddenly turning to a roar, and then I knew the trees were no longer swaying, for now there was only the sound of leaves skittering down the street. In my imagination my girls were somewhere else; like the leaves, they were running down some street, tumbling free through the air, nothing in front of them but the end of the day, the sun losing its strength and beginning to slip into the freshwater sea, the sky becoming a deep, bruised purple. Even though their brother had died three years ago, it was a relief to see their faces not marked by questions; a kind of abandon, a letting go or falling, was written in their eyes, across their smiles, something in their reading beginning, perhaps, to shape their dreams. It was good to let the leaves skitter away. Watching Begé turn another page, Marita stopping her hand, going back to the last page and pointing with great excitement, I felt something like a finger striking my chest, and it was as if my heart leaped to meet the force of that finger, my heart beating strong with the recognition that on the other side of Lorime's death something might await my daughters.

Begé raised her hand and looked over the top of the book. She pulled it close to her chest and smiled at me. I waved, she waved back and then stood up, the book still against her chest with one hand, and with the other she pulled down the edge of her skirt. Marita looked to the window. I waved for them to come outside into the light and warmth of the afternoon.

One Wednesday evening I walked a thin path through the oak woods between the library and Central School. The trees had now lost most of their leaves, their naked branches filled with the guava light of the setting sun. My dark blue flats rustled through the crisp leaves, the evening air beginning to chill, the tip of my nose cold and wet. Every Wednesday evening, from four thirty to seven thirty, there was a farmers' market in Central School's parking lot, just off the edge of the woods. I had told the girls that after school they should go to the library, and then I gave Begé fifteen dollars, told her to put it somewhere safe, and that at five o'clock she and Marita could walk over to the market and pick out a few pumpkins to carve, and a peck of apples. If the Salvadorans were there with their stand, I'd told Begé, buy two *pupusas* with the money that was left so they wouldn't go hungry. I'd bring some caramel and sticks from the grocery store.

Something about the path—how smooth and worn it seemed, and the spaces between the trees—stopped me. It all seemed so familiar, as if I had just walked through these woods and along this path that morning, or dreamed it the night before. The trunks of the trees were distinctly marked by their bark, thick and cracked like strong rope, the evening light between the trees pink and orange, a gauzy blue mist rising from the gold and red and brown leaves carpeting the ground.

This is where he had been. These were Lorime's trees.

I squeezed my coat pocket. I felt it—the moment rose in my mind like a brief movie or dream. Lorime's teacher must've brought her class to this grove. The winter before, Lorime had asked for a dollar. He came home one day with a small paper bag, and he then spent a good part of each evening just inside the door leading down to the basement, sitting on the second or third step, a weak bulb overhead, slowly sanding a block of wood so smooth it seemed to turn bone white. He would never tell anyone what it was for. Someday, he'd say, someday you'll see. And there were days I waited, looking, waiting to see what would rise—a butterfly, a hummingbird, an orchid—right out of that block of wood.

I could see more: Lorime's teacher brings some old sheets out here, and in a few plastic pails she pours varnish from a gallon can. A sheet is ripped into strips, and each student is given a strip of cloth. Lorime crumbles his into a ball, dips it into a pail of varnish, and then begins rubbing the varnish over and over into the block of wood, trying, ever so carefully, to follow the grain, until the block becomes a deep darkened brown.

I stepped closer.

Lorime would've been here, too, hugging a tree, smiling in that safari coat, as his teacher took the photograph he would glue and then shellac to the block of wood.

I pressed my palm against the tree, the bark cutting into my skin, and I felt the tree's imprint. The trees darkened around me, the mist holding scraps of blue as jays screamed through the branches. I heard laughter, clapping, the strumming of a guitar, and then song coming from the farmers' market. A tree seemed to blaze with fire—a cardinal flittering in its branches. I pulled my hand back, touched Lorime's block of wood, and stepped back on the path, on my way to find the arms of my girls.

He looked too disheveled, the cuffs of his jeans creased and splattered with bits of white and pink, a long yellow stain running down the front of his double-breasted blue jacket. There were little anchors on the gold buttons, and given that he wasn't wearing a shirt, his collarbones brown and hard, the jacket seemed strange—like something that he might have found in the bottom of a box, or on the side of the road. The blue wool somewhat faded. He had a small purple button-pin in the lapel, graced by two white Chinese characters. I did not know his name; he lived in a little house behind our apartment, and every once in awhile I'd look out my window and see him in the backyard reading a book.

He bent over quickly, his eyes clenched tight, some sharp pain coursing through his body. He had his wallet open, and when he opened his eyes he started to cry, his voice low and filled with some kind of deep sorrow. The young woman waiting on tables stopped. Placed her hand on his shoulder, and asked, Are you okay, professor? Tears welled in her eyes. They stood there looking at each other in a way that suggested they might embrace. He pulled a credit card from his wallet, dropped it on the bar, and said, Oh, I locked my keys in my car and . . . it's been a bad night. He choked on a sob, and then wiped his face with the back of his hand, stood up straight. Thank you, I'll be fine, he said. I'm going outside to wait. Will you bring out my order?

She nodded, the order pad trembling in her hand.

The bartender handed me a small coffee and a plain bagel in a paper bag. I walked out thinking how close the professor and the waitress suddenly seemed to be, the way her eyes became clear and attentive and concerned when she recognized him, first perhaps a little shocked by his appearance, and then worried as he bent over in pain; and even though her words were distant and formal, and she did not call him by a first name, they seemed to share some sudden intimacy.

When I reached the alley I stopped, stood very close to the building. Peeking around the edge I watched as he paced in front of the deli, his hands deep in his jacket pockets, the shoulders tight, the front open, revealing his chest and stomach for a moment. It was a bright spring day, the morning air chilled, a robin loud in a patch of grass underneath a blooming tulip tree, two sparrows fighting on the edge of the curb over a piece of thick, torn bread. The professor ran his hand through his hair, sat down on a chair next to a bistro table. He leaned back, looked up

into the trees, and when his shoulders started to shake he folded
his arms over his stomach and then bent over and retched with
dry heaves. I turned away, my hand at my mouth, my back against
the wall, a nauseous wave tumbling my stomach.

Alberto used to call most Sundays. He talked to all of us, telling us about a beach or a place in the mountains, how he went
to a festival and heard some great music, or ran into a long-lost
cousin or a childhood friend. And always how warm it was, how
he didn't miss the cold, the thought of another winter. Then
cards arrived instead of calls, some small notes. He didn't return
when I expected. Two weeks past his return date, and he still
hadn't. He wrote a small one-page letter saying he found a job, at
a tuna factory, and it paid much more money than he could ever
make in Niles. He included a check for $300, and I was surprised.
Soon more money arrived, $250, $100. Then $200 in an envelope
with a photograph. Alberto on some walkway along the sea, leaning against a black railing, his hair thick and curly in the breeze,
not quite smiling. A few puffy clouds in the background, the sea
choppy with silver waves. Not smiling but his face tan and clean
and thin with an assurance I hadn't seen in years. The young
Tito I fell in love with there against the rail. And then the money
stopped. No more letters or notes. Never again a phone call.

　　Tito was twenty-one when we married, and I eighteen, and
after nineteen years of marriage, my thin wispy body in that
lemon-yellow dress I wore for the ceremony—standing in the sun
with the Brooklyn Bridge in the background, my hand shading
my eyes, the other holding a bouquet of white flowers, my new
wedding band shiny on my finger—that body, that Maria, seemed
to disappear. The next day Tito and I boarded a bus for Michigan
on our way to his waiting job at the Green Giant cannery, and
somewhere along that flat, never-ending highway I must've
begun to lose the need to shield my eyes from the sun. We went
years with no choice but to scrimp, and once we started to have
children there was never quite enough of anything, food, clothes,
money. Tito had one job after another—working the line on the
night shift of the cannery, on a crew keeping up the irrigation
pipes in the pickle and tomato fields, all day long cutting wings
off chickens in the meatpacking plant—and in a town that never
cared whether we lived here or not. For ten years we lived on a
dirt road that dead-ended against the railroad tracks, a road of
migrant shacks, trailers, and a few two-bedroom ranches, about
a block from the cannery. Little Pea Road everyone called it. The

cannery actually once owned the road, and they built the original shacks so the men who came to work there would have a place to sleep. Little Pea Road: We've fallen so far, we're peas without a pod to piss in, the men used to say.

For ten years we stayed out there, along with most of the Puerto Ricans who lived in Niles, and a few Mexican families, all of us feeling it best not to give up this place along the edge of town. When Marita was born we had three children in a two-bedroom ranch, maybe 650 to 700 square feet. Spring to early fall it was fine—we spent so much time outside, the kids running on the dirt road, playing in the backyard, and just outside the kitchen door, Tito had built a small kitchen of blocks like back home, with a flat cement counter, a grill, and a little area for an old washer and dryer, a clothesline running from the kitchen to the back of the house. We put a picnic table next to the kitchen, in the shade of two short oak trees, and a small bird feeder that filled in the early morning hours with sparrows and robins. Sometimes, in late August, a hummingbird might appear out of the blue, its wings furious in the hot gold light. I'd spend the whole day out there, preparing an evening's meal, doing laundry, sometimes sitting at the table with the children as they colored and read, Marita swinging in a small hammock between the oaks.

During the long gray winters we couldn't remember summer. We were too crowded, too loud, always bumping into each other when the kids were home from school. It was Tito who finally said it was time to move. In the evenings he would circle ads in the paper, and I'd bring home addresses from the library's bulletin board, and he'd go into town and look. Some landlords told him we had too many kids, others said we didn't seem to have steady enough work. Tito would become quiet, drawn into some place I didn't know, and then his face flushed with a hard grimace, not quite anger and not yet disbelief—something he couldn't seem to name as his jaw clenched. He told me it was like begging to live where dogs wouldn't live. Dirty, drafty, dumpy little apartments. Eighty-year-old houses that hadn't had a repair in who knows when. And they don't want us there. They don't want us to live in their houses, Tito told me.

When I told Tito he should go back to Puerto Rico for a visit, maybe I gave him permission to never return. He went to visit family he hadn't seen in over twenty years, to eat a cold coconut *helado* in the midday sun, to stand in the late afternoon in a downpour as the earth turns into a thick dark sea filled with the smell of bananas, orchids, and rain, and to stroll down the pathways of a park just before dark. Lorime's death had changed Tito's life in ways I couldn't seem to grab hold of. It wasn't just the drinking, that he went for weeks drunk, and then became so sick as he sobered up I thought he'd shatter with his shaking, only to then gather the strength to become quiet and distant, spend long hours sitting in the backyard. He'd have the manila envelopes out there with him under the tree, and the photographs: Lorime unrecognizable; his nose cut and blue; his eyes swollen purple; his cheeks bright and fat like rotting apples; his hair too black, too greasy, feathered back from too much blood. Some days Tito would be gone all afternoon, and all he could say was, Ah, I was walking along the river.

Somehow it came out, someone must have been close by and witnessed what happened, that the four young men who beat up Lorime were laughing and yelling, calling him a greaser, a queer, a little Puerto Rican pea. When he died that same night of internal bleeding, I sat next to his bed repeating his name, Lorime, Lorime, Lorime. I said, My son, remember, and I watched Tito sitting there with his face in his hands, his elbows digging into his thighs, as he rocked back and forth and his insides heaved, his collarbones rising and falling.

He told me many times how it was all his fault, that he should've never moved us to town away from Little Pea Road.

That's what change gets you, he said.

I had no choice: I had to tell Tito to go. I couldn't bear to see him sitting underneath that tree, the manila envelopes in front of him, a bottle of rum next to his leg, his shoulders shaking like brittle dead branches in the wind. I sometimes tell myself that I understand why he stayed away, why he might never return. Maria, I tell myself, he must miss his daughters; and then the questions begin, how can he just forget them? Daylight, nightlight, when does he remember me? What color shirt is he wearing, and how does it ripple in the breeze? Then I stop the questions, because in asking them I look up to the sky, and then there comes hope even in the smallest cloud floating by. Maria, I say, it's been three years, and you can no longer try to create memories of Tito for his daughters. They have what they have, all they'll hold close.

It's been almost a year since anyone in his family has seen Tito. The last time he was living near Ponce, working at the port. No one can find him there anymore.

Maria, who knows, maybe Tito went for a long walk along the port one warm evening, the palms rustling overhead and breaking his shadow into tiger stripes, the sun a globe of fire beginning to fall toward the sea. He squinted, raised his hand to his eyes, and then he walked a little farther and got on a slow boat that disappeared to where only the sun's flames know.

Just the other day, on the radio, there was a news story focused on a family hurting from the raid. A seven-year-old boy, who was staying at his aunt's apartment, didn't know what happened to his father. When his father never returned from work, the boy stood there by the window, in that apartment above a pizza parlor, looking down on the sidewalk. His crying—his voice high and scratchy, filled with tears—had been recorded when the reporter visited, and edited into the news story. At times I never heard what the reporter said; the crying in the background was enough to bring me the news.

The boy's mother was there in the room talking to the reporter. She said she just wanted to know what had happened to her husband, where he had been taken. That first. And then, of course, that he would come home. The news story never offered any names; the mother did not want to be picked up, and she agreed to meet only because she wanted others to know that people like her husband were taken away to who knows where, and four days after the raid her son still cried. She had what others might think a silly hope: somewhere her husband would hear her voice, and then find his way back home.

The sunlight now falling through the kitchen thickened within the grains of Tito's photograph, the sea bluer, choppier, crested and more the sea. I liked the hardness of Tito's cheeks, how the lines on his face seemed smoothed by the yellow light above the sea, that same light drifting around my chair, across my hands.

I know that pizza parlor and that second-floor apartment. I pass them often on my way to work. The smell of rising dough is strong, and sometimes I look up as I take a deep breath, and on the second floor I see white lace curtains swaying in the open window. I wonder if it's hot up there, if maybe for them the smell is not as startling and new, the smell does not evoke the hunger that rises from the deep pocket of my stomach as soon as I encounter it on that sidewalk. And then I say, No, there's more hunger there, Maria, than many of us will ever know. I imagine Tito, far away, somewhere still alive with his hunger. And though maybe I shouldn't love him, I hope that wherever he is, he's discovered peace, he has an open window and swaying curtains.

The professor, Luis Manguel, had strung café lights along the garage roof, and there in their light Pablito, his son, ran in a skeleton costume, the bones a green glow in the darkening evening, a plastic pumpkin caught in the crook of his arm. There was a small fire in the *chimenea*. His backyard seemed blanketed with soft gold light. The girls and I made our way over, Begé holding a platter of caramel apples covered in cellophane, Marita with two pumpkins in need of carving, and I with a small pot of red beans in tomato sauce with smoked pork hocks, and a bowl of white rice. *Never, ever, arrive for a parranda without food,* I remember my mother telling me, and I found myself laughing inside, because that afternoon, when I saw the professor and his son walking down the sidewalk, tossing a small football between them, it was so easy to say hello. He said hello, too, and introduced himself, Luis Manguel, and his son, Paul, and then he added, Pablo, Pablito.

That's my name in English and Spanish, he said, his light brown hair lifting in the breeze as he held the football up to me.

I took it from him and squeezed the middle; it needed some air. There were red and green dragons on the ball, and then words like *Welsh* and *Scotland*, and I realized it was not a football at all but a ball for rugby. I looked at Luis and asked, Not professor? His face lit up like a question mark, and then he smiled.

No, Luis is fine. But how did you know?

I see you outside, in the backyard, sitting with a stack of books for many hours. Sometimes in shorts, sometimes in a shirt with your tie loose, and I thought, He must be a professor at the university. Who else would spend so much time reading?

His face flushed, but then he smiled again, and said, Yes, I am. English, writing and literature.

Maria, Maria Arguadas, I said, and put my hand out. We shook. Sometimes I see you . . .

I looked up into the trees, turned down to Pablito, handed him the ball.

My kitchen window looks out on your backyard, and I see you sitting in the evening with your lights and your fire, and you read until it must be too dark to see.

Pablito leaned his head against his father's thigh, and Luis gently cupped his hand around the side of his head, and then he said, I hope I'm not hurting my eyes, but I like the quiet, the way the light turns blue and marks the end of a day.

Always you are alone, and now for the first time I see you with Pablito.

Pablo's visiting for a few weeks. He lives in North Dakota with his mother, and I sometimes visit him, but now he's here.

Oh, I said. I don't know why, perhaps because I suddenly felt embarrassed in asking about his life, but I said, My girls and I are making caramel apples tonight, and we're going to try to carve pumpkins.

We are too. Well, we were going to carve some pumpkins out back, make some hot chocolate. Why don't you join us?

I ran my hand across Pablito's head. Yes, we'll come over, the girls will like that very much, and I bet they'll like meeting Pablito, I said.

Cars now made their way along Sycamore Street, the sound of their tires humming in the evening air, over houses and trees; then leaves lifted from the grass and fell with a crinkly hush. Pablito ran up to us, his pumpkin bumping against his thigh.

Hola, he said.

Hola, Pablito. I'm Maria, we met before, and these are my daughters, Begé and Marita.

Look, see my pumpkin? Pablito held it as high as his arms could reach.

Nice, Marita said.

Hello, Maria, and then I turned to the back of the house, Luis stepping out in a dark blue sweater over a white T-shirt, a pair of jeans, and sandals. I raised my arms, beginning to grow heavy from the beans and rice. Let me help you with that, he said. I handed him the pot of beans. I could smell his aftershave, a citrus mix with perhaps bay leaf, and then I thought I smelled frying oil. His hands were streaked with flour, a few spots along the bottom of his sweater. He smiled when he saw me looking at the spots.

Fried chicken, with pinches of sea salt and Spanish paprika in the flour—that's Pablito's favorite. He could eat it day after day.

Sounds delicious.

I've made enough for everyone. What do we have here? he asked, holding the pot higher.

Red beans and white rice, I said, shaking the bowl.

Ah, one of my favorites.

We were standing on a small wood deck, not that high off the ground, the platter of caramel apples and the pumpkins on the deck seeming to float above the grass. There was a very short, small table of wood, and two chairs of the same wood— weathered, gray, and looking just like the pallets Mrs. Sanchez's groceries were delivered on.

I see you are admiring my furniture.

Yes, it's interesting.

And you're probably guessing correctly—yes, I made it myself from pallets. Here, sit down. Try it out.

He went inside. I sat down, tentatively, as if the legs might fall out from underneath me. Surprisingly, they felt strong, and comfortable. Luis returned with two glasses of white wine.

I have soda, juice, water—but would you like a glass of wine?

I raised my hand and took the glass he offered, thanking him. I asked him why the chairs and table were so short, small. He sat down. He told me that he had lived in Spain for a year; he had accepted an offer to teach at a university in Madrid one fall, and then stayed on into the spring and summer, mostly reading, thinking, traveling. He made a little bit of money by tutoring *madrileños* in English. In the small, almost cavelike *tabernas* he liked best, where the air was cold and strong in the warm afternoons, there were these short stools and tables, as if, at first, one were almost sitting on the floor. But then they became more and more familiar—and comfortable. With a glass of brandy or wine at his side, Luis could linger over a book, some writing he was beginning.

Those stools and tables became second nature to me, he said. He paused, looked out on the children playing next to the garage with Pablo's rugby ball, then closed his eyes. He took a sip of wine, and I raised my glass to my lips. He replaced his glass on the table, rubbed his eyes, and when he opened them they sparkled, and I thought his eyelashes looked wet.

You see, Maria, Paul, Pablito, had just turned two before I left for Spain, a job and trip I had never intended. His mother and I had lived apart for several years, because I couldn't find university work close to where she worked, Grand Forks, North Dakota. She had a great job then, at the university, a home, and then Pablito was born. I found good steady work in Minneapolis—tenure-track, lifetime work, I thought, the kind of work where I'd never have to worry about money again. I commuted, traveling back and forth as often as possible. We thought what we were doing was best for Pablito. Now, when I look back, I see we did nothing for our marriage, for each other. One day, Pablito's mother, Lydia, told me, basically, she no longer needed me in her life. I did what I've always done—shut down, accept things for what they are, beyond my control, and so I burned bridges. Cut all ties, made it difficult to find me. I must have worked, eaten, slept—and yet I remember none of it. I drank a

lot. Walked around in a daze. Then I quit my job. Put my books
in storage, sold or gave away my possessions, and then, through a
friend, found myself headed for Spain.

So Pablo was two?

Yes.

It must have been hard, at that age, to be away from him.

Absolutely.

He stopped and then tore off a small splinter from the end of
his chair's armrest.

You know, he said, the parks—with their playgrounds, their
fountains and benches—are wonderful in Spain, a real family
affair, and there I was: all alone. I missed Pablito greatly, his
mother too. Before I went to Spain, when I used to drive into the
Grand Forks region to visit them, I'd suddenly feel the car filling
with the smell of potatoes cooking in the processing plants, and
my stomach would dance with butterflies to see them both.

He smiled, took a long drink of wine. Enough, no?

I shrugged my shoulders. Then I asked, curious, How did you
then make him a part of your life?

He looked down on the deck and then quietly told me how
one night he took a chance and called Lydia from Spain. He simply asked her if she and Pablito might visit. There was a long
silence on the phone, and then she said yes, and even though she
had said she didn't need Luis in her life, she never meant for Luis
to think that Pablito didn't need him in his life. They visited. Luis
took Pablito to Valencia on the train, Lydia staying in Madrid.
They walked along the beach, Luis held Pablito in his arms as
they floated in the sea, and in the evenings he'd push Pablito in
his stroller down the brightly lit cobblestone streets. When they
returned to Madrid, they all spent time together—at the park,
sitting out on a terraza with some drinks, Pablito loving fried
baby calamari.

Ah, I should get the food soon, no? Luis pointed to the
children.

I shrugged again, not wanting to say yes—his voice, the
memories, spoke to me in ways I couldn't quite understand, something like the quiet feeling of the fall wind catching itself underneath my hair, moving slowly along my neck. His voice different
from my own: his voice calmed my talking inside. I knew loss,
and I recognized how I always counted losses, as if in doing so
I knew where they ended. In the calm from his voice I felt there
would surely be more I needed to accept. Like leaves falling out

of reach, tumbling down the street, and never slowing down for
me.

Luis, did you hear about the raid?

Yes. He looked down into his glass for a moment, then said,
Yes, it is all very sad and confusing.

I think I know what you mean.

It doesn't make sense. I can't understand what the govern-
ment is thinking, ruining all those lives, tearing apart those
families.

The sky turned a deeper blue, the edges of dusk branching
out into the trees. I heard a voice from the university stadium, the
words loud but incomprehensible with echo on the loudspeaker.
Luis had heard of the parents taken into custody, what had
happened to the children when they were separated from their
parents.

Did you hear the story on the radio of the young boy, seven
years old, waiting for his father? I asked.

Yes, I did. He gripped his knees, tightly, and then said, In
Spain it was different. There were no raids of factories or con-
struction sites. But anyone who looked saw the workers who
had migrated there: everywhere they carried bricks and lumber,
pulled sacks of crumbled, broken debris out onto the edge of the
sidewalk. In the morning, in the night you saw them ready for
work. They were helping to build a new, modern country. But
it was clear—in the newspapers, on TV, on the streets, and in
the tabernas—that many did not want them there. Temporaries.
They could work and live for a time. They needed them to work.
But they needed them to go back.

Luis took a long drink of the last of his wine. Then he said,
The day of the raid I was bringing Pablo here from his mother's.
On the radio they were announcing the possibility of raiding the
meatpacking plant. It was strange, and later, when the raid was
described, I wondered why so many went to work on that day.
Did they not hear the news? And then I thought, maybe they live
every day with the fear of raid. How could they not show up—
they needed the work. I said to myself, work is what they knew,
and even if they heard, they simply went to work feeling that
maybe the raid wouldn't happen.

I shrugged, unsure of anything to say. I could see how
unsure Luis was too. He said, Pablito and I had been driving since
first light, and the countryside was thick with green rolling hills,
tall grasses swaying in the breeze, and every so often a red barn
would light up a field. I saw streams I hadn't expected, shade

trees along their edges, then a line of cows making their way to a stream. They announced on the radio that the authorities had set up holding cells for the arrested at the county fairgrounds. I was just imagining how fortunate Pablito was to grow up in a region like this, and then it struck me so hard: for such beautiful countryside, I couldn't understand how it harbored so many betrayals.

I started to take a drink of my wine. Stopped. My hand trembled for a moment, and I put my glass down. Begé and Marita laughed, chasing Pablito as he ran around the yard, his arms raised high, his orange pumpkin over his head. Then I squeezed the art project in my sweater pocket. I pulled it out, held it in the deepening dusk for a moment, and placed it on the table next to our glasses.

My son, Lorime. He was seventeen when I lost him three years ago. I guess it's an art project, from when he was young.

Luis picked it up, turned Lorime toward the starlight, smiled.

I can't stop wondering why Lorime never brought it home. It was found in a shoebox—all those years, and I never saw him in this picture.

Happy. He's happy here in this moment, Luis said.

Yes, it is so clear, and it makes me happy to know that.

I started to cry, couldn't seem to catch my breath, and then bunched my hands underneath my arms. Luis placed Lorime on my armrest, his bright, young face smiling. Luis squeezed my shoulder for a moment, and when my hands came down he took my left hand and held it with firm warmth. My girls were standing next to Pablito, his pumpkin and rugby ball on the other side of the yard, and I heard him say, *On your marks, get set, go*. I wiped my eyes, looked at Luis, smiled.

Tell me more, Maria, tell me the whole story. *Cuéntamelo*, Maria.

I know it's impossible but maybe Lorime wanted us to have it now. Maybe he wanted us to see it on a night like this, I said without an instant of pause. My chest rose for Begé and Marita and Pablito out in this evening air—here under the growing light of stars emerging just before dark—breathing in whatever was offered, feeling, deep in the small and fragile borders of my heart, that it came with a sorrow I could never betray.

FINCA

There seems to be only the foundation, the cracked and weather-softened pylons, a small rusted flywheel. A silver stream running alongside, catching against stones, foaming white, the stones suddenly tiny mountains shrouded with heavy mist. The banks overgrown—bushes, passion fruit vines, a flamboyant tree, some wild bananas. A molasses factory. Here cane boiled to syrup and bottled. The shell grayish brown, the planks of wood worn smooth from hard sea winds, the tin roof wrinkled, torn in places, and covered with leaves and dried cane stalks. Walls have collapsed. A chinaberry tree has taken root on the main floor, growing without care through a star-shaped tear. Most of the windows are propped open as if the kettles are still boiling turbulent rivers of steam, smelling earthy and dark, almost sweaty with work, the men in their smudged-brown whites and jagged straw hats raising their dark arms, the silver slice of their machetes setting the cane free in one sharp, decisive, crystalline cut.

Steam, a dark green broken by egglike hills of red clay dirt, a team of white oxen lumbering across a field, their silver haunches powdered with dust.

My father's story coming and going without shape or sound as the seasons changed and the stream rose, roared, overflowed its banks, receded, then disappeared into a dry pebble-strewn arroyo of silence. Sitting on a Coca-Cola crate, his blackened hands dipped into a wood bowl, spooning rice into his mouth. Like little pearls brought up from the deep of a cool sea filled with iridescent scallops and shells, oysters and clams, and the red seahorses, he once told me, that galloped on silver-crested waves on those late afternoons that seemed beautiful, *elegante*. The tin roof hot and shiny with the day's ending.

The sea breeze softly shakes the windows. I still listen for the mill, wait to hear it turn with the sound of the stream gurgling over stones, the mill turning out deep dark molasses, generating electricity for the lights strung across this stream, these lights lighting up the green black night—like pearls, scallops and shells, oysters and clams, a seahorse's vermilion wake the stars marking the night's voyage.

ACCEPTANCE

My mother folded my shirt collar down, smoothed the lapels of
my coat, and then straightened my tie one more time. She folded
a handkerchief in half across her knee, doubled the fold. Knelt
down in front of me, small streams of winter light entering the
room, she folded each corner into the center until she had a small
box. She turned the points of each corner into the center once
again.

This is a man's rose, Ernest.

The sun—like thick clouds of gray light swirling through
the window—caught across the tops of her hennaed hair, as she
tucked the man's rose into my breast pocket. This was the ritual
of her dressing me: the stiff shiny shoes, the crisp cool cotton of
the hand-washed shirts, the smooth halo of the tie, and then the
feel of each and every loop of my waist, the tight cinch of my
belt. My arm searching through one sleeve, then the other, followed by the slide of the black jacket over my shoulders.

In the early mornings of the fall—after the Cream of Wheat
the orange juice the sweet coffee—I take my books and my
mother's hand, and we step on the bus. All the men in boots, their
metal lunch boxes, newspapers tucked under their arms. The
click of the women's heels. The half-light of morning still soft
and puffy with the night's neon and the silver of the bus gleaming on storefronts. My mother lightly squeezes my knee, and I
pull on the chain overhead. I leave the bus, hurry inside the gate,
and walk under the tall oak trees arching over the walkway, and
though I'm only nine years old, my stomach is awash with waves
because I did not touch my mother's cheek one last time. Walking
through the ivy-covered doors, I step into the brick building and
pass rooms bigger than our house, each room lined with endless
rows of books—the sweet smell of leather, gold letters like
sprinkled dust across bindings, and the skinlike feel of a book in
my palms. All the other boys with their black ties, their bright

white shirts, and their shiny shoes clicking down the long hall-
ways on their way to class.

This was the first time my mother had given me a man's rose,
and I accepted it as a new part of my mother's love. She was the
one who created the everydayness of my life. The school suit
I wore—she worked deep into the night, a single yellow bulb
throwing light away from the rapid fire of the sewing machine.
Her hand coaxing the black wool, pulling and cutting thread, the
light brilliant across the top of the black bobbins, her hair.

On Sunday mornings, her hair powdered with flour, her skin
gritty and smelling of butter and dough, long loaves of French
bread and a red ball of cheese tucked under her arm. Saturdays
she worked the night shift—eleven to seven—at a French bakery,
rushed home with my breakfast, slept a few hours, and then took
me to mass, followed by my favorite part of the week: our few
hours at the Fox Library. We sat at a back table, near a window, a
white birch shaking in the wind, and read a book together, her red,
chapped hands slowly turning a page when I squeezed her knee.

Now my father swung the bedroom door open. My mother
smoothed down the shoulders of my coat, one hand running
down my spine, the other along my chest to my stomach. My
mother and father didn't say a word to each other; they lived in
worlds as far apart as continents divided by a sea. In her eyes she
said, *You are the night and I'm the day.* In his eyes he said, *You are
the fresh water and I'm the oil.*

My mother rose from her knees, smoothed down the front of
her turtleneck sweater; my father leaned against the doorway, his
hands fidgeting in his jacket pockets. She stepped to the window
and looked out into the weak late-fall light.

Changó, my father, took my hand and we walked down the
hall and went outside. We crossed Reed Street, stepped into the
field, and slowly moved away from the house my mother and
father rented from an Italian contractor, a house on the edge of
West Hartford amid factories and loading docks, the backyard
filled with scaffolding and cement mixers. The field my father and
I walked across was a testing ground where the asphalt factory
rolled out their trucks and steamrollers, the air heavy and thick,
the men covered in tar, the blue of their uniforms like little ponds
dotting a landscape of deep black soil. They laid down strips of
asphalt, the outcomes of the factory's formulas, the experimental
births of parking lots and driveways, roads and highways.

The field was now empty. The ground was cracked in places,
olive weeds growing through the asphalt, and, in the distance,

some bushes and a small oak tree. The sounds of our feet, the silences between, it was the same every Saturday afternoon: my father left angry, hurt, feeling helpless, because no matter how hard he worked, there was never enough money, and he couldn't help pay for my schooling. We'd leave and give my mother the afternoon and evening alone, a chance to rest before her night shift. Sometimes my father and I would walk and walk, Changó driving his frustrations into the pavement. On warm days he'd take me down to Bushnell Park, where the men sat on milk crates and played dominoes on a makeshift table. Changó would bring a paper bag and pass it around. On rainy afternoons we'd sit in the high-back leather chairs of the Auster Hotel, my father thumbing through a Spanish newspaper while I drank a chocolate malt and looked out onto the city. Most of the time we'd head for Park Avenue, Little Puerto Rico, the music, the food, our relations.

We crossed the road, away from the field, and walked along a dirt embankment, above the sewer stream flowing in from Hartford. Lined along the bank were chunks of gray stone and white boulders. Following the stream, looking toward Hartford, the tenements arose in the darkening distance, a few windows gold with light. Changó turned up the road, toward the bus stop on New Britain Avenue, the Mr. Donut on the corner.

The donut shop was luminous inside: the stainless steel coffee urns a pool of silver, the red seats in front of the counter floating above the smooth, clean floor, the glass cases lined with neatly placed donuts, some sprinkled with coconut and colored sparkles, others glazed or dusted with sugar. A woman in a white uniform and a pink gingham apron asked what I would like. She drifted behind the counter, slid open the glass case, reached inside, and pulled out a powdery donut. She took an off-white cup, placed it on a saucer, and filled it with hot chocolate. The cup balanced on the saucer in her hand, in her other hand the donut, as she came back to me in her white shoes, her white stockings, her sandy-brown hair.

Somewhere, at the Fox Library, in a book at school, I had read of a woman named Diana, the name on the silver badge pinned on the left side of her apron. Diana sitting by a stream and waiting. Someone for whom ancient battles were fought. Through the glass I saw my father walk around the corner, his hands deep in his pockets. He shrugged his shoulders as if in apology, his face flushed and a cigarette dangling from his lips, the smoke turning orange in the neon. I turned away, bit into the donut, and took a sip of my hot chocolate. My father acted as if I never knew, but I knew, I could tell; there was always a bottle hidden under the couch, behind the refrigerator, or underneath the front steps. Here, at the donut shop on New Britain Avenue, it was the same—Changó went to the package store across the street and bought a bottle, or went next door to the bar, the bottle already half empty and hidden within his jacket, and as the night darkened he'd turn to the bottle more and more.

The bells on the door jingled. I felt his heat against my back, my shoulders. Changó's warm breath against my neck, around my ear, sweet in my nose. His whisper: *Ernestito, let's go.*

Changó's arm crossed my shoulder, his hand stubbing out his cigarette on the saucer, ashes and tobacco mixing with my donut's powder.

The night air was chilly against my back. The windows of the Mr. Donut started to fog. Diana was bent over, leaning her elbows against the counter, her right hand holding her hair. My father smiled, put his hand in his pocket, and handed Diana some money. I could see her face, her lips—*Thank you.*

Changó stepped into the chill of the night. He shrugged with a shiver, opened his silver lighter, and lit a cigarette, the purple flame caressing the sides of his smooth cheeks. He snapped the lighter closed, slid it into his pocket. Raising his hands to his collar, he pulled it up, his long black trench coat snug across his broad shoulders and cinched into a V at his waist.

Changó called me: Ernestito, *escúchame.* He put his arm around my shoulder, his face serious, and then once again he began to tell me about the white ox chained to the mill on the outskirts of the cane field. Sometimes red dust rose from the deep path the ox had worn into the ground. Sometimes the path was filled with rainwater, the ox's belly wet and gray with rain. Changó never spoke of the tiredness in its eyes, the sweaty, rippling skin of the ox; he struggled to unload the heavily stacked carts of cane, his back tightening, his biceps swelling, his thighs trembling. One night, with all the boys and men resting around a fire, he felt something hot and sharp well up within his chest, a force like a strong afternoon sea breeze striking a palm tree—and he was suddenly singing, composing the *guaracha* "The Dance of the Tired Ox." He was singing, dancing with a strange joy, and he was suddenly nothing: he was not sea breeze, palm tree, or cane field.

My father seemed sad, as if something had left his body and he might disappear into the neon lights that glowed on his face, in his eyes. Then he smiled, laughed, twirled in place, and raised me into his arms, into his warm, sweet breath, his strong arms.

Ay, Ernestito. Dance with this tired ox.

We took a bus down New Britain Avenue away from West Hartford, past Colt Park and the yellow, wet-looking streetlights, the bus circling onto Capitol Avenue. The sidewalks looked slick underneath the gold dome of the capitol washing onto the streets and gutters, reflecting back into the tall Greek columns of the Bushnell Theatre.

We got off the bus. Changó leaned against a phone booth and lit a cigarette. The flint wouldn't strike. Finally, the purple flame, Changó pulling deep drags. He walked away, smoke trailing over his shoulders, I following behind, knowing it was beginning: sometimes he seemed happy, open with his love, his words, but then the rum made him blind, angry, silent, like a tired animal trying not to fall. He tried to turn the corner, bumped into the side of a building, staggered for a moment, caught his stride, and turned onto Park Avenue.

My face tingled in the sharp wind, my toes numb within my stiff shoes. My father walked ahead of me, caught for a moment in white, a bright circle of light falling from a dented green lamp shining against his black coat. I heard music and laughter, the inner vibrations from the Club Coqui spilling out onto the sidewalk. My father slowly took the steps and went inside; he made his way toward the bar. A lone lightbulb hung over a picture: a *coqui* frog sat on a green leaf cut in the shape of an island. Under a heat lamp there was a piece of pork turning on a spit and a paper-boat holding *papas rellenas* drifting in grease. The window fogged in waves along the bottom, and the warmth of the lamp and the pork came to me through the glass.

The door slammed open. My father yelled, tried to push his way back in, but the man told him, *No, no mas*, his arm across the door, catching Changó's throat. Changó swung, but the man grabbed his fist and pushed him off the steps. Changó crashed against a paper machine.

The man looked at me and shook his head. He turned, stepped inside, and yelled for everyone to leave.

Three men descended the steps, their heads hanging low, giggling as they looked down on my father.

The door slammed shut and I heard the lock click with a hard shove. The music died. The man who had pushed my father cut the pork into the paper-boat and shut off the heat lamp. I watched him drift away through the darkness, across the image of the coqui, his shoulder brushing the light, the gold light swinging, splashing the black room in soft waves.

I turned to my father, bent over, took his outstretched hands and tried to help him up. I let go, his weight too much. There was a warm shadow on my back. Underneath the lamp, the collar of his dark brown leather coat pulled high around his ears, stood my father's cousin, Boogaloo. He had one hand tucked into his pants pocket, his other hand pinching a cigarette between his lips. He took a final drag, pulled his cigarette down, flicking it against the sidewalk. He smiled.

Don't worry, Ernestito, we'll get him home.

Boogaloo walked forward, bent over, and lifted my father into his arms. I heard him whispering but the only word I recognized was *Changólito*, and then my father's hands seemed to suddenly grip Boogaloo's shoulders tightly, a small whimper rising from his throat. Boogaloo told him it was time to go home, and he raised my father from the sidewalk.

Soon we'll all go home, Boogaloo said, looking at me. Puerto Rico, no?

Boogaloo dusted off my father's trench coat, tucking his tie inside.

Changó's ready to go, *hijo*, but he must take it easy or he'll never arrive in one piece. He waved for me to step forward. Boogaloo stood on my father's left and I on his right, and trying to keep him in between us, we made our way down Park Avenue.

We walked for an eternity down the dark streets, Boogaloo's cigarette a red eye, my father bumping back and forth between us, and then we finally turned onto New Britain Avenue: the street-lights fluttering in a gold stillness, the bare trees black upturned hands grasping for stars, the quiet houses falling asleep in my mind when a front porch light blinked off, the wind stopping for a moment, the flag next to the front door slowly becoming soft and still. Boogaloo's hand on my head, and as he rubbed the back of my skull he said, Don't worry, hijo, it'll be okay.

My father mumbled, sometimes whimpered, seemingly unaware that he had a son walking next to him, stumbled unaware of the emerging rhythm inside his son, the music turning over and over into a future memory—*This is what it feels like to be a tired ox.*

Boogaloo soon got us on a bus, and we were home in less than a half-hour.

I opened the front door. My mother was asleep in a chair, her legs wrapped in her housecoat, a sweater draped over her shoulders, a book open on her lap. Her hennaed hair curly with exhaustion. After Boogaloo put my father to bed, he opened the front door and headed for the street. My mother called to him, Boogaloo, don't go. And then she said, *Manuel*—the first time I heard that name—Manuel, you don't have to go. Boogaloo stopped, his hand on the doorknob. He let go, turned around.

Don't leave, Manuel. It's late. I'll fix up the couch.

Boogaloo stared at the floor. When he raised his head, he said, No, I don't want to bother.

Please stay; it will be good for Changó. In the morning he'll find you here, and he won't feel alone, my mother said.

Boogaloo said he'd stay, then, for my father and because she asked, unbuttoning his coat and handing it to me. I turned, walked into the kitchen, slipped his coat on the back of a chair, and went down the hall and up the back stairs to my room.

The silence of the house turned the air around me electric. I could hear the steady hum of the refrigerator; a car slowly turning some corner and then speeding up; the wind rising with some great force, as if the ocean had come with it, leaves crackling against the bottom of the house, the wind caught in the swaying trees, a branch tapping the roof in a steady rhythm. I focused on the thick blue air in the back field outside my window, through the twisting and blurring black branches. How deep and tangible it seemed, because for a moment it became a dark ocean of waves rolling with the rhythm of the tapping branch, the bright windows of the distant tenement building bobbing in the waves. My feet were still cold, and my hands trembled. I couldn't sleep. I rubbed the bottoms of each of my feet along the insides of my calves, my flannel pajamas warming them slightly. I wasn't sure if the wind stopped or if it was the loudness of her voice—perhaps her heart, some deep longing I still don't understand—my mother crying, Boogaloo saying, quickly, It's okay, Evelyn, okay, okay.

The furnace kicked on, a rumbling rush of heat rolling through the vents, and I did not hear either of their voices again. My heart rose heavy and loud in my chest, my ears burning with blood, and the branch continued to tap against the roof.

Feeling the warm waves of heat filling my room, I lay down on my bed, my eyes tearing in the sharp air, in that sudden strange state between wakefulness and the need to sleep. I knew—it was like an instant image or scene in my eyes—that my sleep would be restless; in a few hours, or maybe just before dawn, I would sit up and pull my shirt over my head and wipe the sweat away from my neck. I'd walk to the window and pull it up with as much strength as I could gather, a rush of cold air against my stomach. Pulling the blanket over my legs, I tried to push myself into sleep quickly by creating a memory, a little dream story of things to come that were clear and calm. I dreamed tomorrow, Sunday, library day for my mother and me. We sit together at a gleaming oak table, a book opened flat in front of us, and in our separate silences we both follow a boat twisting its way along a deep brown river, gnarled groves of trees along the banks, the shrieks of colorful birds broken every so often by the boat's sputtering engine. Our knees often touch under the table, and whenever my mother taps my thigh, I reach over to take the cheese sandwich or cup of sweet creamed coffee she smuggled into the library inside her raincoat. As we read, her voice rises in her throat, a hum of pleasure, and wonder I catch in the solid attention of her eyes, her fingers pressing into the page, and I read the words again searching for the intimacy she's discovered, waiting for my voice to rise with the same urgency she seemed ready to accept.

Outside, the wind blows, a leaf strikes flat against the glass, and I look at the tree sway without regret.

THE SHADOWS OF PALMS

Abuela Monsa stands in her open kitchen. Steam rises with the
little song she hums. She dances and sways to her song, moving
back and forth from table to stove. Sunlight slants into the doorway, banana leaves shaking in the breeze, shadows entering in
waves behind the sunlight and the leaves. A hummingbird flutters
just above her shoulder, its ochre throat turning silver against the
color of her hair. She works between this morning's shadow and
sun: she chops garlic, onion, green pepper, cilantro, and tomato.
She adds them to a pan of simmering rice. Pouring achiote oil into
the pan, the rice turning a deep yellow. She lightly rubs the side of
my cheek with the back of her hand, smiles, and then turns over
a small blue bowl, a stream of glistening gandules trembling into
the pan. She spoons coffee into a boiling pot of water, then adds a
small cup of cream and a couple spoonfuls of sugar.

The kitchen: the doors wide open, windows without glass or
screens, leaves and hummingbirds freely floating in, the sunlight
filling the kitchen and patterning the white tiled floor with the
shadows of palms.

The salt, black pepper, olive oil, and the sweet smell of mangoes ripening on the table. The lush shaking of leaves, fruits
hitting the ground in a deep thud, abuela's sandals scraping the
floor, her spoon striking the side of a silver pot: *Why is it now
filled with such silence?*

Abuela brings me a cup of coffee, a plate of yellow rice and
gandules surrounded by slices of avocado. This old woman, her
flowered dress, her silver hair, her dark skin a calendar of sun
falling into the sea. My first memory of my father's mother. The
first time I tell myself, *Run a sharp knife across your palm, feel the
small living gestures that count the most.*

FIRST LOVE

I was reading on the front porch when I heard Ernest and his father on the sidewalk, their shoes scraping under the mulberry trees, and as I looked up from the page they ducked under the drooping branches, their shoulders brushing against each other. Ernest slipped off his suit coat, folded it over his arm. He waved. His father, Changó, stopped, lifted a plastic bag, shook it and smiled a broad grin, his face red in the sun, bits of tissue soaking cuts, the spot under his bottom lip still dark and in need of a shave.

On my lap, wrapped in soft and crinkling green paper, were half a dozen pink and white carnations I gathered with baby's breath for Ernest's mother. My best friend, Ernest, I had drawn together the flowers to show him I felt how much he missed her. I closed my book, lifted the flowers, and waved them in a hello.

Stepping up onto the porch, Changó came to my side, his thigh firm against my shoulder, and I looked up as he squatted next to me. He opened the bag over my lap; inside was the pink and blue carcass of a rabbit.

Tonight, Magda, Ernest's cooking soncocho, he said.

I turned from the bag, my nose crinkling, shaded my eyes and tried to smile. Turning to Ernest, I stuck out my tongue and found myself shivering at the thought of the rabbit cut up in pieces and floating in a red stew, chunks of potatoes, diced green pepper, onion, cilantro.

Changó leaned back, laughed, his teeth shiny in the sun. He looked at me and rubbed his stomach, licked his lips, a quiet hum lifting from his throat. He raised the rabbit from the bag, the carcass a bright pink, the muscles along its little legs blue, the white bones showing from where it had been cut just above its feet. Changó suddenly broke out in a small two-step, waving the rabbit in the air. Ernest folded his coat over the porch rail. Changó slipped the rabbit back into the bag.

Magdalene, your mother inside? Changó pulled a pint of rum from his coat pocket.

I nodded.

I take the rabbit inside then?

Go ahead, Changó. No worries—she's at work.

He touched my shoulder as he passed, pulled open the screen door.

Hey, Ernest. I stood, smoothed down the front of my new yellow dress. I picked up my book, pressed it against my side, folds of gingham gathering on my hip.

Ernest smiled, stepped forward, his hand stretched and shaking. We greeted each other with our fingertips.

Rabbit stew tonight? I asked.

Ernest began to shake his head, but then we both laughed. He raised his hand, his fingers gently rubbing the little curve inside my elbow. He must have ironed his shirt; the white flat and crisp, and his black tie patterned by a tight weave that looked elegant. His brown hair was feathered back, and his face seemed fresh, awake, and even happy for a change.

My stepfather pulled into the driveway, stones crunching under the truck's wheels. He stepped out, his blue shirt drenched with sweat, his green paisley tie wrinkled and loose around his neck.

I jumped down off the steps, my Mary Janes scrunching when I hit the driveway's stones. I opened my arms, threw myself against him and held him tight, the smell of whiskey and cigarettes strong, his wet shirt clinging to my palms.

How did it go, I whispered.

He separated from me, both of his hands on my shoulders.

Not much to expect, Magdalene. I think it's over with, even for me. He ran both his hands through his hair, closed his eyes, let out a deep sigh, his teeth gritted together, grinding.

Many had already lost their jobs that year. A company from Toronto had bought the cannery, and their main concern was the growing of mushrooms. They planned to bring in an East Indian foreman from Toronto, and his task was to make the new changes; no more canned mushrooms, only the round, fresh white ones, my stepfather had said, packed, and shipped out—all from the squat concrete buildings where the mushrooms were grown. My stepfather had been out there for three days trying to save the cannery, arguing with the new management, fighting to keep the corn or pea line, making the case for all the jobs that would be lost.

He pulled out a cigarette, tapped it against his thumb knuckle quickly and hard. It bounced with a leap from his thumb, and he caught it in his lips, lit it, and dragged deeply, the graying hair around his ears wet with sweat.

Thanks for taking us to the hospital, Ernest said.

My stepfather pulled his shirttails from his pants, nodded. No problem, pal, it's the least I can do. He took another drag, exhaled. Looked down at the back of his hands, he rubbed the long scar along the knuckles of his right hand, seemed to separate from us in an instant, thinking, arguing, remembering.

A few days before, Ernest and Changó had helped bring him home. The sun had just dropped past the trees on the other side of the river, and I started to shiver, my shoulders and nose burnt from the day's warm May sun. Changó's laughter startled me, and I turned to the street, and then I was shocked by my stepfather's harsh words. *Fuck 'em all,* he said, *and the horses they rode in on.* The tips of his boots scuffed up the steps as Ernest and Changó helped him make it to the porch. I heard my mother open the screen door behind us. Changó caught the edge of the door with his shoulder, and then it was as if he and Ernest paused, gathered some strength, and pushed my stepfather over the threshold. Inside, they laid him down on the couch. He swung his fists wildly, striking his own shoulders, his ribs. His arms suddenly fell quietly to his sides, his eyes closed, and I heard him whisper something like he was sorry, so sorry, Changó, for he had never wanted to let him go. We all looked at him—his unshaven face, his lips slightly parted, the bits of yellow rice stuck to the left side of his chin. Changó lowered his eyes, and my mother turned to him. I couldn't look at the anger in her face, and when my eyes met Ernest's, I waited for her to start yelling. Surprisingly, she never did, even though she never had a kind word to say about Changó or Ernest.

The silence of the room seemed to deepen with such a heavy weight as we listened to the dam in the distance, the sound of the river pounding the rocks below.

And then the quietness drifted away, changed into the thick rays of golden red light from the setting sun filling the living room, and for the first time—out of all the years of my mother's bitter rage—I saw her hands shaking at her sides.

Ernest turned to the door, and my eyes burned with the awareness that at thirteen years old I had nothing to do or say. All I could do was cry as quietly as possible as I ran to the back of the house and my room.

My stepfather now smiled, his thumb raising up and his hand bouncing in a greeting. Changó stood on the porch; his face flushed, his jacket off, his black tie tight around his neck, the knot a little crooked. He stepped forward and his feet seemed to bump against each other, and then he swiftly caught his stride from the stumble. From his shirt pocket he slipped out a pair of sunglasses and, with a slow, graceful flourish, slid them on his face. He took a long drink from the pint of rum. He passed it to my stepfather.

Ernest held my hand, briefly, gave it a squeeze. I wiped the sweat from my forehead, the porch beginning to become too warm. I picked up my book and the flowers, and we walked to the truck, my stepfather and Changó following behind. They sat up front. Ernest got up into the truck bed and spread out an old wool blanket for us. My stepfather backed out of the drive-way, headed down Third Street, and then turned west on Niles-Buchanan Road. The air filling the bed was warm, but I felt a cold pocket deep inside, something left over from the beginning of spring, or following the winds from far off on Lake Michigan. I thought of how an ice-cold pop burned going down my throat, how on a warm evening after a bike ride with Ernest along the river, I welcomed the burning pain, how thrilling and new it felt each time I raised the bottle to my lips, the bottle slick and cold in my hand, and when I looked at the gurgling pop I felt that chilled burn catching in my throat.

For a moment my eyes fluttered with that sensation, and when I opened them wide Ernest had his hand in his hair, his head tipped back against the bed of the truck, his eyes closed, the sun catching bits of gold and red in his hair. His mother's pain had to be different, even more intimate and yet strange, shaped by her bleeding throat.

We crossed the river, and in a brief space of sunlight I caught a glimpse of Island Park. There, in the twilight, Ernest had told me that when his mother came home from the hospital, after her tonsillectomy, she and his father had fought. Changó was pacing around the living room, wearing a circle into the rug. His friend, Boogaloo, had called about factory work in Flint, and since Changó hadn't found a new job, he wanted to go. Ernest's mother—her voice hoarse, her face pale—had said they couldn't talk about it now, that he needed to wait, see what happened with the cannery. He sat down at the kitchen table and opened another beer, took a shot of rum. He opened his suitcase in the middle of the floor, unpacked it, and walked around some more. Then he pulled Ernest's ear, told him to repack the suitcase.

Ernest was silent for a moment, and we watched a mallard duck wobble up on the island with her brood of eight ducklings, their yellow-and-black down looking soft as it ruffled in the breeze. He said that Changó had all the lights in the house blazing, the stereo on. Evelyn couldn't sleep and asked him to let her rest. To just wait for another day. Changó started to yell, screamed about a new life, money, how he had to go. Ernest didn't listen to it all, and he said he just wanted to tell Changó to be quiet, to go out for the night. When he moved to separate them, he didn't make it in time. Changó turned, smacked his open hand against Ernest's forehead, his palm driving his head back, stopping him. Changó picked up the suitcase, swung it behind his legs, and threw it. For the first time he saw his father striking out at his mother, and he couldn't do anything as the suitcase flew through the air, his mother raising her arms slowly, the suitcase hitting her chest and spilling open. Her head struck the doorjamb, and Ernest ran and caught her before she fell to the floor.

Now she was in the hospital again.

The next day his mother awoke as if nothing had happened. She walked gingerly to the car but said she would take Ernest to school, even though he wanted to walk. As she drove, she shielded her eyes, her other hand gripping the wheel tightly, her knuckles as white as her face. They were almost to school when she started swaying in her seat, humming and moaning. She slowed, pulled to the side of the road, and threw up. Ernest got out and brought some paper napkins from the glove compartment. There were thick splotches of blood on the road. He said they were like tomato sauce, and he thought he saw bits of her throat. She choked and coughed, and the napkins he gave her quickly soaked with blood. He didn't know what to do. He couldn't lose the image of her bulging eyes, her white and purple face, the edges of her lips streaked with blood. She fell against the door, and then into the road.

Niles-Buchanan Road dipped and curved, and my book slipped from my lap. I picked it up, held tighter to the flowers. I motioned to Ernest, patted the space of blanket at my side. The truck straightened, and he crawled over and sat next to me.

Up front, I watched my stepfather and Changó in some deep conversation; they laughed, pointed at a fresh-plowed field, the earth black with tiny flecks of silver. Changó took a drink and then passed the bottle to my stepfather. The dogwood trees and lilac bushes were in bloom along the road, purple and white blurring with the thickening green woods. White blossoms fluttered in the breeze, and I followed their patterns as they landed in my hair, on my lap, the truck bed suddenly filled with the scent of lilacs, the wet river, fresh-cut grass.

I saw her hennaed hair first; will always remember how it curled against the bright pillow, how it tinted the white hospital room. Her face thin, her lips drained of color, and her bony, dry hands above the sheets, her fingers pressed into the cloth as if she were clutching two apples. She smiled at Ernest. He walked to the side of her bed, bent over, kissed her on the cheek, and then with his left palm he brushed her bangs off her forehead and kissed her again, her wrinkled brow smoothing when Ernest lifted away.

Good to see you, Ernest—here, she whispered, help me up.

Ernest slid his left arm behind her shoulders, slowly lifted, taking his mother's weight against his chest, and with his free hand placed two pillows behind her head and shoulders, and then laid her back gently. Her face bloomed with color, the tip of her nose a rosy red, petals of purple rising on her cheeks, and she seemed happy we were there.

I walked forward from the door and handed her the bouquet of flowers.

Oh, thank you, Magdalene. She cradled the flowers and took a deep breath, her eyes closing for a moment.

My God, these smell like heaven. She opened her eyes, looked at me, her eyes first meeting mine, holding them for a moment, and then taking in my hair, my shoulders, the cut of my yellow dress and how it shaped my hips.

Come here. Come closer, Maggie.

My heart rose against my clavicles, hard with its shaky beating. She asked me to turn around, and I did, the hem of my dress rising slowly. She motioned me closer, held me, the scent of rubbing alcohol rising from her gown. She took a white carnation, snapped off the end, and tucked the flower into my hair, just above my left ear.

Changó stepped forward. His eyes were pooled with tears, and he bent over as if he wanted to hug her or lift her from the bed—but he stopped, his hands behind his back. He turned to the window, stepped closer, and looked outside. He lifted the empty beaker on the windowsill, brought it back to her bed, unwrapped the green paper around the flowers, and slid them inside. He filled the beaker with the water at her bedside.

Thank you, Changó. They'll live longer now, Evelyn said, her hands raised to her neck, her fingers gently massaging the skin.

Please put them in the window, she whispered.

My stepfather sat down in one of the chairs in the corner of the room. His hands were on his thighs, then he raised his left hand, waved. I stepped next to Ernest and gently gripped his shoulder. We leaned against the wall. Changó sat down in the other chair, next to Evelyn's bed, and crossed his right leg over his left.

I heard birds outside, imagined them chasing each other in the thick pines throwing shadows against the window. Evelyn looked up, but Changó didn't say anything, only looked down at his hands, which slowly trembled before he clasped them together and dropped them on his lap. He couldn't seem to sit straight, shifting from side to side. Finally he looked up and asked, You doing better?

Evelyn shrugged, leaned her head to the right, and whispered, Better.

The door opened, and the doctor walked in, scanning a clipboard and then writing something very quickly. He stopped, turned the pages of the clipboard flat, looked around the room before focusing on my stepfather and Changó.

Mr. Arroyo?

Changó sat up straight, unclasped his hands, and his left index finger slowly rose in the air.

The doctor stepped forward, the clipboard behind his back, looked down on Changó.

Evelyn is not ready to go home today. She's lost a lot of blood, and what she needs is rest. No talking, no work, nor any stress. The doctor's face flushed with the word *stress*, his jaw set hard.

Changó held the edge of chair between his open legs, his fingers tightening. He shook his head.

You understand then? The doctor's eyebrows raised with the question, and he didn't seem to wait for an answer but turned to Evelyn, asked her to open wide, and started to look down her throat. There's good improvement here, he said. But we want to see much more. He wrote something on his clipboard. He nodded and then began to make his way from the room. He stopped, turned to my stepfather.

I think it would be best, and I hope you agree, that she doesn't have any visitors for the next few days.

My stepfather lowered his head for a moment, raised it and stared at the doctor, a frown on his lips.

The doctor stepped through the door, and I turned to the small whimper coming from Changó. His shoulders shook, and he crossed his arms in front of himself and tucked them under his armpits. Evelyn looked to the window, the flowers bright in a stream of sun and shadow.

Changó bent forward, began to cry softly.

I followed the puffy shape of sunlight clouding the water underneath the flowers; bits from the stems circling near the bottom of the beaker. My mother wouldn't come with us today, although she always said Evelyn was an old friend. She needed to go to work. She enjoyed her rides to and from Berrien Center, she often told me, found a great sense of comfort driving down the long country roads lined with apple and peach orchards, fields of asparagus and celery, and the bright blue patches of blueberries she'd see in late June. Depending on the season, there were different colors, changing scents she'd gradually learn, and she could choose various routes, never having to drive into the same cannery parking lot. Even though she worked for County Family Services in a green trailer on the edge of some potato fields, dealing day in and day out with the paperwork or presence of migrant families, she said it made her world brand new to get away. I wondered what she had seen on that morning, if she'd had a glimpse of the same kind of light that fell on Evelyn's hair.

Ernest moved to his mother's side. She raised her right arm and held his waist as he bent over and gave her a kiss, a brief hug.

Changó rubbed his hands flatly on his knees. He stopped, raised the backs of his hands to wipe his eyes.

What was it that brought his anger and love to these tears? What was all the fighting about—work? A job? Not living in Puerto Rico? Why couldn't he stand up and look at Evelyn, maybe even tell her he was sorry. I couldn't see my stepfather throwing a suitcase at my mother once he was let go from the cannery. There wouldn't be anger or violence in our house— silence, more silence, would touch our lives. They'd sit out in my mother's garden, drinking coffee, listening to the twilight rise until their silence became the dark of night.

In my room I'd hear their chairs creak, maybe my mother blowing on her coffee, my father tapping a cigarette against his thumb. The click of his lighter. The river falling over the dam in the distance, the hollow sound of logs knocking against each other on the edge of the paper mill. The silence would fill my room, and when the mill's whistle blew for the start of the night shift, I'd have no choice but to remember how my life was shaped by work. My father, like my mother, came to work at the cannery, migrated from the East Coast to take a chance in answering a call for workers. I never met my father, never knew if he had been one of those recently let go by my stepfather, or if he had left to work and live somewhere else long ago. If he had forgotten me. His migration never failed to take me to a region beyond the silence, some place I still needed to discover.

I touched the flower Evelyn tucked in my hair. Stepping to the right side of her bed, I touched her forearm, squeezed her wrist. She smiled. Whispered, Take care of him, Maggie. Just like always, be his friend.

I turned away because I knew that the silence of that room was much better for Evelyn than seeing me cry. I thought I heard, *Remember that for always.* I followed Ernest out into the hallway, and we walked down the shiny pattern of white tiles toward the exit. A group of nurses stood at their station, the doctor talking to them. They were in middle of some anecdote, some joke, giggling. They turned silent when we passed, and I wiped my eyes, stared at the floor, and clasped Ernest's hand.

It'll be okay, Ernestito. Two, three days—what do they matter? They'll go by fast, and then it'll be like she was never gone. He squeezed my hand and then rubbed the back of my thumb with his own.

There was a loud scream. We turned. Inside a room, lying face down on a bed, a little boy screamed while a woman held his hand. A nurse looked up, moved to pull the curtain—yet we were already staring at a doctor sticking a long needle into his spine.

Ernest let go of my hand, moved ahead of me shaking his head, and then sprinted off down the hallway. I called him, chased after him, and when he slammed through the exit door and it flew back at me, I had to stop, my arms not strong enough to push through. I calmed myself, let him run, and as I smoothed down the sides of my dress I told myself everything was going to be all right, that Evelyn had to get better, and soon she'd be home.

I'm sorry, sorry, I am sorry. Maybe no one could say it, maybe they still needed to feel its truth, and as I counted to ten I waited for something other than words to move through me.

Outside, Ernest stood behind the truck, his fists clenched at his sides, pacing back and forth in a small square, his face wet. I stood in front of him, blocked his pacing. He looked at me, angry. I licked the tip of my index finger, held it in the air for a moment, and just as he started to smile I ran it down his nose, the only gesture I knew to assure him everything would work out okay.

We walked down the frozen aisle, our arms clasped together as if we were marching in a parade, Ernest's left hand guiding the grocery cart. We had gathered for the soncocho a green and red pepper, a bunch of cilantro, a garlic clove, a sweet onion, a half pound of potatoes, two cans of tomato sauce, and a bottle of red wine vinegar. We had also picked up a bunch of bananas, and a pound of rice. I let go of Ernest's arm and bent over the freezer case.

Why don't you fix a pizza one night while your mom's gone?

Sounds good, Magdalene. Tonight soncocho, but maybe the next night you can come over for pizza, he said.

I put the pizza in the cart. Ernest grabbed a half gallon of milk from the dairy case, a quart of orange juice. He held up a package of shredded cheese.

For our pizza, he said and shook the cheese.

At the end of the frozen aisle, just before we turned for the registers, there was a three-tiered shelf of day-old baked goods marked down 50 percent. There were boxes of powdered donuts, cellophane-wrapped brownies, a bag of chocolate chip cookies, some whole, some crumbling. My eyes became full with the wide and flat birthday cake; it had curvy yellow flowers all over the top, daffodils in a field of thick white cream frosting, and then circled in black, on the edge of the daffodils, a baseball, its threads a bright red. *Happy 9th Birthday, John!* was written in green cursive, and on each side of the salutation was a blue fish and an orange bird. I don't know for how long I stood at that never-picked-up cake, and why my mouth seemed to fill with the soft and sweet frosting. Ernest touched my elbow.

Magda, Magda.

I looked at him, felt myself blushing.

He raised his hand and tucked his mother's flower back into my hair, his fingers grazing my ear.

That cake will go good with vanilla ice cream, don't you think?

Yes, I said, and turned back to get the ice cream.

When Ernest placed the cake in the bottom of the cart, I didn't worry that he might be spending some of his father's last money on a cake they didn't need. It felt right. I felt a small moment of richness and perfection as I placed the ice cream next to the cake.

We both took a side of the cart's handle and pushed it to the open cashier. Next to the register, Ernest grabbed a package of hard butterscotch candies and placed them on the belt.

We found our fathers sitting on milk crates, drinking quarts of beer vaguely disguised in paper bags, next to a paper machine. They both had their ties off, my stepfather wearing Chang6's sunglasses. He laughed listening to Changó's story. Ernest stepped forward and gave Changó his change. We walked back to the truck, lifted the sacks into the bed, and then Ernest helped me up.

We got milk, ice cream, frozen pizza, I said. Let's go, Dad.

He lifted his right foot off the ground, shifted his weight on the crate. He lifted his beer and shook it in the air.

Almost done, Magdalene. The milk'll keep.

Ernest had the butterscotch candies on his lap. He motioned for me to sit down. I moved some of the dogwood blossoms away with my foot before I sat down. He began to open the candies. He stopped, touched my thigh, squeezed it. He handed me the half gallon of milk, and I held it as he twisted off the cap. He pulled the edge of the cake box from the sack, lifted the top. He held three fingers up and then dug them down into the edge of the cake. The inside of the cake was yellow, and the frosting looked so soft, as if it were melting on his fingers. He took a bite, pointed his head toward the cake. I dipped three fingers into the box, the cake and frosting smooth and cool, sticky and light and sweet when I took a bite. I let the cake melt in my mouth for a moment, closed my eyes, a fish jumping from a flat lake. I took a long drink of the milk, my teeth tingling, the coldness in my throat making the cake fall sweeter down into the deep pocket of my stomach. Ernest moved closer and drank from the milk. We leaned back against the truck, our fathers behind us, and we waited. Ernest started laughing, pointed. He wiped his hands off on the blanket. Then he reached up and wiped the frosting from my chin, licking it off his fingertips. I wiped my hands on the blanket, looking at the curlicues of frosting on the tip of his nose, on both of his cheeks; and then without any sense of pause kissed the tip of his nose, his cheeks. We lay back, our hands in the folds of my dress, looking up into the early evening sky.

My mother was standing on the front porch when we pulled into the driveway, her arms folded across her chest. She waved, her face without expression. My stepfather stopped the truck, stones flying up and tapping against the front steps. My mother turned and went inside. Ernest and I stepped down, and my stepfather leaned in the back and handed Changó and Ernest the bags of groceries.

You going to be all right tonight? my stepfather asked.

Sure. Ernest shifted the groceries in his arms. Thanks again for taking us.

The screen door slammed, and my mother stood on the porch.

Did you forget this? she asked, lifting the bag with the rabbit. She stepped down off the porch, walked to Changó, and then placed it inside the grocery bag he held.

Cuidado, she said. Please, take it easy, Changó. Evelyn'll be back home soon. And she reached out and touched Changó's bicep, the closest I'd ever seen her near him. She said, We will all lose something soon. And she was no longer looking at Changó but at my stepfather. She paused, her eyes steady, her hands poised in the blue light between her and my stepfather.

You can't drink away whatever you are missing, what feels so important. She crossed her arms. Then she said, I went to see Evelyn this afternoon, after work.

My mother turned to me, touched my cheek with the backs of her fingers. The flowers are beautiful, Magda.

Looking at Ernest she said, And she's anxious to come home, I think. I told her not to worry.

My mother fluffed the curls along the back of her neck.

Can you come over for dinner tomorrow, Ernest?

He nodded.

My mother put her arm around me, and my arm found its way around her waist. My stepfather made a quick salute to everyone and headed inside. Ernest and his father turned away and walked into the mulberry trees, the branches heavy with the sound of birds.

Five years passed, and I would've never remembered my mother's words, or that rabbit, had it not been for Ernest's memory. We were sitting on the Bond Street Hill in the twilight, across the street from the Ring Lardner home. We were counting how many salmon rose before the dam, each fish like a silver sickle cutting through the falling water. I was leaving for the university in two days, and I had expressed that I wasn't sure about leaving, had all these questions, wondered the most if I was going only to fulfill my mother's long dream. Ernest listened and didn't say, at first, anything one way or the other. Then he told me about cooking the soncocho that night. He remembered the two plates of white rice on the table, two glasses of water, and his father's bottle of rum. He spooned from the pot two pieces of rabbit—a thigh and piece of breast—onto his father's plate, a few potatoes, and two spoonfuls of the red sauce. His father didn't speak, the house quiet with the rumble of the refrigerator, the birds chirping in the backyard. His father ate steadily and greedily, draining his water, and then filling his glass with rum. Ernest raised a piece of meat to his mouth, took a bite, started chewing, and was about to say something when he felt his throat close up tight, his mouth half open. He lifted his glass and tried to take a big swallow of water. He hit his fist against his chest, coughed, went over to the sink; he coughed again, turned back to Changó, who was taking a long drink.

The room must have become blurry on the edges yet distinctly clear to Ernest—the bare beige walls, the pieces of linoleum peeling back off the floor in places, the rusty ends of each chair, Changó's elbows up on the table, his chin in his hands, as he looked at Ernest perhaps in the happiness of his meal, or perhaps in a state of disbelief. He must have gotten up and walked over and struck Ernest over and over again on the back. Then all he could do was wrap his arms around Ernest's stomach and jerk, Ernest belching, coughing, and a small bone falling into the bottom of the sink.

With school beginning, the fall would soon arrive. Yet that evening the air was hot, muggy. I was wearing a bikini top and pair of shorts, my back slick with sweat, my breasts hot. A trio of mallards rose over the birch trees.

I remember Ernest telling me that later Changó had come to his room with a small bowl of ice cream. Ernest had said, no, he only wanted to sleep. You need to eat it, Changó told him, and Ernest ate the ice cream quickly. Changó placed the bowl on the dresser and lay down in bed with him. It was warm in the room, every once in a while a quick shot of breeze lifted the curtains and struck the bed. Ernest said he couldn't sleep the whole night, only floated between Changó's memories and dreams, his crying out . . . *No–no–no—*

He'd seem to fall asleep, then suddenly shudder, hear Changó cry out, feel Changó hold him tighter, each of them wet with sweat.

I could see that blue-black room, feel the weak breeze stirring the curtains, and I imagined some dark harmony of resolve surrounding them.

Ernest dug a small hole in the ground with the end of a stick. He looked toward the dam—fifteen, he said, now sixteen, seventeen—and then we listened to the water falling and watched for more salmon to rise. Finally he said, It's not a big deal, but you know my father, somewhat, Magdalene. He's quiet. Maybe selfish. He doesn't seem to want to talk in Spanish or English. I can't seem to remember a time when he ever talked to me for more than five minutes. What happened to him that night—my choking, realizing that my mother almost died? Ernest broke the stick in half, flung the pieces away from the hill.

For some reason, Magdalene, I know he was trying to express something. Ernest leaned back, his hands clasped behind his head.

I leaned over, kissed the top of his clavicle, the inside of his neck, and then rested my head on his chest.

The shade started to brighten with sun, Magdalene, and I slipped from Changó's arms and walked out to the kitchen.

Ernest told me how there was such an immense, bright emptiness. He stood behind his mother's chair, held it, and cried because he had this strange feeling there was something pushing him toward the moment when he'd walk out of that kitchen for the last time.

When he said that, my stomach dropped, and my arm raised from his chest, hovered for a moment, until I consciously wrapped it around his torso again, held him tightly. Without the memory of my father, I wondered when I'd ever have a night when I felt that strange harmony, my father's love.

There's nothing wrong, Magdalene, in wondering what's brought you here, he said, running his index finger along my arm. Or knowing it's time to go.

The day after Ernest had cooked the soncocho, when I stood on the sidewalk outside their house, I did not know of Ernest's choking. I had a book bag leaning against my leg, two towels tucked under my arms, and when Ernest stepped onto the porch I waved a hello with my head, my hair tied back in a yellow ribbon. All I wanted—all I thought of—was reading together down by the river, taking a swim once the afternoon turned hot. Ernest hopped down the stairs.

Wait—Ernestito, wait. Changó stepped through the screen door, his pants half zipped, the buckle of his belt striking his right thigh, his belly and chest glinting in the morning sun.

Ernest took my hand, said, We're going down to the river. I'll see you later.

Changó lowered his head, then looked at me, the towels.

Come, Ernestito. Just for a minute.

I let go of his hand, nudged his hip, and he then walked up on the porch. Changó said something, and Ernest stood behind him and stuck his hand in Changó's pockets, pulling out some dollar bills. He slipped a few into his shirt pocket and then slipped the rest back into Changó's pants. I heard him say, Here, Changó.

He stepped closer, grabbed the front of his father's pants and brought both sides together, catching the clasps to each other. He pulled the zipper up. Holding the buckle, Ernest brought the leather end through, buckled his father's belt, tucking the extra leather through a belt loop.

He stepped down from the porch. I waved good-bye. Ernest lifted the book bag, swung it up and slid his arms through the straps. We walked down the sidewalk and cut through a vacant lot, the tall grass itchy on my ankles, on our way to Bond Street. I could hear the dam and followed the sound of a boat heading upstream. Through the trees I looked down on the river, the water rippling gold in the sun, and the smell of lilacs came to me strong and clear.

Ten years have passed since Ernest's mother came home from the hospital. The cannery closed. Mushrooms were grown. Evelyn and Changó separated for at least three years, and then they returned to each other with a love I can't easily understand. My mother was right—we all must've lost something. We made do, ate from her garden more often, made it bigger. My yellow dress became a summer top, and the extra fabric helped to cover a hole in the seat of my stepfather's truck. The company from Toronto eventually closed down their operations. My mother and stepfather grew closer, sometimes spending long afternoons driving down county roads my mother remembered. Ernest left for South Bend, then, I heard, Chicago, yet I have a strong feeling I'd recognize him anywhere, even with the knowledge he'll never be—*remember that for always*—my same friend.

The Royal Café sign finally flickers off below my apartment. The smell and taste of coffee still thick and warm, the edges of my windows wet with the heat of the roasters. I sit in this sudden, new darkness wondering what it feels like to be held so closely you feel your breath tighten, disappear as your eyes sparkle, and how blue the air seems as you choke, your throat hard and thin, your hands alive and trembling in the colored air you gasp for.

Once, under the blinking marquee lights of the Ready Theatre, I saw Evelyn and Changó embrace with such force, Changó lifting her from the ground, Evelyn's shoes hanging off her heels, and my shoulders suddenly burned with such fire I thought I'd lose control of my stepfather's truck.

Here, in this university town, I discover moments that help me remember what Ernest felt that night; he made it sound so frightening, Changó so smothering and forlorn, a feeling so strange and foreign, a place existing at such a far distance I knew that a voyage toward its shore was filled with risk. Thrilling, almost magical loneliness in that room changing into something else. Here, I have a futon mattress on the floor, a desk with a lamp, a typewriter, a chair, and piles of books arranged on the floor, against the walls. I look at the three-by-five cards I need to fill, the sheets typed on the desk—it feels too crowded, and I search for a way across the distance.

Remember Ernest standing on the edge of the mulberry trees: his shirt clean and pressed, and his hand rising with a thumbs-up as my stepfather drove down Third Street, my mother sitting next to him, and I in the truck bed with a suitcase by my side on my way to Ann Arbor.

I wipe away the moisture from the windows with the bottom of my shirt, the cloth cool against my belly, my thighs chilled with goose bumps. I raise the middle window higher and look out onto the empty street. If it is true that only a handful of men migrated to Niles for work, the women who also came may have been a few fingers on a hand. Sometimes I think about going back, I think that after five years I can apologize for my absence, my silence. Mamí, let's go for a drive, I'd say. I'd drive her to the cannery, and together we'd look out on the green fields, and then take in the crumbling buildings where the mushrooms were grown, the fallen roofs, the sagging fences. I wouldn't point but simply stand still in the blaze of insects swarming in the tall grasses, flying figures filled with shadow and light in the truck's headlights, the dam falling in a fine steady crash to the west, a bevy of bats arising with the darkness and erratically shaping the last bands of dusk. We would look at the front window of the main office, shattered with a gaping hole, and follow the bluing outline of the fallen Jolly Green Giant lying facedown on the weed-choked parking lot, his garlanded head cracked, splintered, white from years of weather, only a few specks of green remaining. I wouldn't ask once again about my father—*who is he? Did you and my father come together or separately? Can't you at least give me a name, a memory?* I'd bite my tongue, aware of the circle of forgetting and anger my mother stood within, and so I could never ask her to tell me about her first love.

Mamí, I know it's hard but tell me your secrets. Can't you tell me at least one? Can't you tell me what you are so scared of? And how, on a night like this, when I've traveled farther away from where you are, I can salve the fright here in this room, here along the edges of my heart?

I move closer to the glass, feel the rusty screen against my palm. Down and away from my room is a line of orange detour signs; they blink on and off, an arrow pointing and then disappearing, the black street suddenly bright, then dark and slick. New curbs. New sidewalks. The curving, changing roads. The rumbling of the compressor running the lights fills the window-sill, and as the glass vibrates, a jerking start-and-stop rhythm fills my shoulders, and I sway back and forth. My hands rise to my neck, help me to stand steady, and I wonder about the different ways to go, the detours we follow, when what is needed is the strength to drive straight through.

FALLEN LEAVES,

YELLOW, ORANGE, GREEN

The dormitories are constructed of concrete blocks. Their exteriors painted white, their rusty tin roofs shaking the men out of bed when the fall rains seemingly drop without regret. They look to be about six and a half feet tall. Lined in even rows—six rows wide, six rows deep—inside the cannery's barbed wire compound. Each dormitory is roughly one hundred eight feet long and about sixteen feet wide. Every odd-numbered dormitory where the workers sleep, every even-numbered dormitory where the mushrooms grow. Two communal dormitories exist: one for showering, the other for eating.

It is night, a silver moon brightening the paths of grass and black dirt between the dormitories. One shift sleeps while another sifts through the manured shelves, eyes squinting in the small circular lights of their helmets, hands adrift in the stench of dirt, manure, and the invisible gas of fertilizer.

Dawn means gray-blue light of dew and mist, green helmets with small lights on their brims passed on to the incoming shift in the twenty feet separating each dormitory. For miles the smell of celery, cows and pigs, wet chicken feathers, pickling spices. Apples softening in the grass. The cool scent of mint and the river smells that fill this ripening, working valley.

In the dawn someone drives by and partakes of an odd, misunderstood ritual: short, swaying arcs of bright light in the deep green field.

IN THE FIELDS OF MEMORY

Tino is a good six corn stalks in front of me. His wrinkled, sweat-stained paper-sack hat knocking against the cream-yellow tassel tops of corn. Deep in the green, up ahead of me, Boogaloo's voice rises from the wet field like the repetitious song of the coqui frog:

> *Que me duele la cabeza*
> *Tráeme una cerveza*
> *Que me duele el corazón*
> *Tráeme un palo de ron*

Then the soft, tired voices—Tino, Arturo, Negro, and my father—sing in harmony the guaracha's chorus, their voices hanging low near the dirt, floating back toward me through the dew-covered leaves. The guaracha is a new lament, a song of sorrow and longing that Boogaloo has brought from a recent, brief return to Puerto Rico. Only fifteen, I work toward this song, I keep listening and try to stay close to the men. They keep moving, the tops of the corn rustling, swaying.

Sometimes the song is all we have—the rhythm that soothes our hands scraping the leaves, lifting bags of potatoes, our feet walking up a dusty lane, stepping behind a tractor in the late afternoon sun, jumping on the back of a wagon.

Sometimes the song is all I have—the rhythm of a language that separates me from the men. It reminds me that I have not lived the lives that they have, that even though I haven't left an island like them, I am too young to be without a home, too young to enter into a lifelong struggle to find work. It reminds me that I should be ten miles down the road, in Niles, going to high school with my friends.

My thighs are sore and chafing in the dew that has soaked my pants. I can't keep up this morning, my arms tired, my head foggy

67

from too much drinking last night. Outside the Sportsman's Bar, I sat under a tree, drinking a six-pack of beer, while the men went inside. Blue and red lights circled within, the deep beat of drums escaping from the swinging doors. I was about to fall asleep when they came with a bottle of cold Don Q, yelling for me. They passed around the bottle, laughed at each other's stories, and played dice. Under the August moon, we walked along the edge of the highway, back to our shack, the lights of cars and semis spraying across our faces, down to our shoes. Single-file, kicking up stones, into the cool darkness we sang our song:

> If my head hurts
> Bring me a beer
> If my heart hurts
> Bring me a shot of rum

Sometimes it isn't enough to work hard and fast, to try and keep up. Some mornings all I can do is stay quiet and wonder if I have no choice but to become the man my father is: silent, always tied to men who have worked since they were children, men who seem to walk with a stoop straight toward death. I wonder if there will always be Boogaloos in my life: men who don't feel any pain. He's full of smiles jokes laughter—full of his voice, the guaracha, and he sings louder and moves faster and faster down the rows.

Rápido, rápido, mis hermanos.

Moving faster, I pull off three more ears, drop them into my burlap sack. Last night, outside the bar, underneath the tree, Boogaloo told everyone how he wasn't going to work in fields anymore. He has changed, and he has returned to live each day smooth and light. With good food and drink. Song, laughter.

Suave.

So rich, hijo, I wipe my ass with one-dollar bills.

My father wasn't angry, and his voice wasn't drunk. He stared into the fields. When his father made him quit school, he never thought he'd leave the fields of Puerto Rico to end up working in these fields. He looked at Boogaloo, and his lips trembled for a moment. He focused on his hands. He said that in the middle of the cane field he felt at peace swinging his machete in hard slices, and that the hardest work was at the mill unloading the carts of cane, seeing a white ox chained to the mill, walking round and round. That ox had walked so much rain filled its path, the water lapping against the bottom of its graying stomach. My father and the other boys never spoke of the tiredness they saw in its eyes. All they did was keep working, unloading the carts, their arms heavy and numb and humming like hot steel. One night, under a mango tree, listening to the fire, dried cane pieces cracking and sparking toward the stars, he quieted the talk of the men and the boys. Changó, my father, made up the guaracha "The Dance of the Tired Ox." The song kept them moving. They lost the humming steel in their skins, the memory of their families, inside that song. Only nine years old, he, like Boogaloo, was filled with dreams. Days went by, years, and now there are no more dreams, now it is as if he has walked into his fate: my father living in the memory of fields.

I break off another ear.

Those were the most words I ever heard my father speak, and under that tree, in the moonlight, as he sang I heard how beautiful the guaracha is, how deep inside, my father has a strong, lovely voice.

I walk out of the corn row to the field lane. Tino jumps up on the wagon—his droopy blue pants frayed, caught on the bottom of his shoes, his shirttails ruffling—and rolls over the mound of corn. He lands on Arturo; Arturo pushes him off to the side. All the men sit in a circle, their backs against the slats of the wagon, on the outer edge of corn. Arturo drops his head onto his knees, wraps his head with his arms.

Hurry up, *pichichi*, Boogaloo yells.

They raise their heads, look back, laugh. Mr. Vollman jerks the clutch, speeding the tractor up the lane. I run toward the wagon, lifting the bag over my shoulder. My father kneels at the end and I throw him the bag, jump.

I don't know what's worse, hijo, you or the *viejo.*

It's only around seven o'clock, my skin soaked, soon the sun rising higher. I will work most of the day with wet, mildewed clothes drying on my body like a wilted second skin: I don't need Boogaloo's mouth poking at me, calling me *hijo.* He may be my father's cousin, but that doesn't mean I have to respect him. He smiles, his face broad, black, his teeth white and straight. He waits for me to say something, but I can't.

My father throws an ear of corn, striking Boogaloo's chest. He laughs, picks it up, and tosses it back to my father, who catches it and drops the ear into his lap. He claps his hands in front of him, then wipes them down the side of his pants. His hair is wet and shiny, his face beginning to turn nut brown. He lifts the ear, pulls back the husk, raises it to his lips, and sucks the juice from the sweet corn, staring at Boogaloo.

My father has told me that Boogaloo's from the pueblo of Loíza, where most of the Africans live. Boogaloo's some Yoruban spirit name, and my father doesn't seem to remember his real name—Manuel Perez—because everyone's called him Boogaloo for so long that the name has stuck. His mother is Iríke, my great-aunt, who I met a long time ago when we went to Puerto Rico. Boogaloo has been a shadow in our lives for some time. But there's this hidden story, some distance between them. I thought I once saw my father and Boogaloo as close, their arms around each other, their pants rolled to their knees, smiling on the seashore in Connecticut. Here in Michigan, though, there's doubt. All the men seem to walk in a dream, seem to forsake who they are, and work for people who treat them like dirt. My father is quiet, foolish, drunk most of the time. He and Boogaloo make fun of each other, cut each other down to the bone, and they don't question a thing, will not yell out or fight back.

My father turns the corn cob in his lips, sucks one more time. He tosses the cob at Boogaloo's feet. He wipes his face with the back of his hand, sucks his teeth, tilting his head back against the wagon slats and closing his eyes, the sun brown and soft on his brow.

When my father laughs I never sense any bitterness—his laughter is like his face: brown, soft, and for a moment not afraid to stare into the sun. There must be something else—*there must be more, some other time.*

We all jump off the wagon. The sun rises higher, prickly warm against the back of my head.

A sunny day, my mother's hennaed hair, standing in a blue polka dot dress, a little suitcase by her feet. She slid her fingers into a pair of white gloves. My father took my hand and turned us away. He walked us down the sidewalk without saying good-bye, without questioning why she was leaving, where she was going.

Tino walks forward, slides open the pole-barn door. I walk to the rear, open the back door. Arturo moves across the hard-packed dirt floor, turns on the electricity, the dusty yellow lights flooding down on the green and black machinery. Now we will leave the corn behind. In the afternoons, under the sharp sun, Tino, Boogaloo, my father, and I stand on the back of the potato picker watching for sticks, stones, potato plants, clumps of soil. Mr. Vollman driving up and down the rows. Negro and Arturo— the strongest, full of stamina, who work like burros—walk behind the picker and bend over picking up any potatoes the

picker has missed, ankle-deep in the soil, kicking up dirt, a gold
stream rolling behind the picker as they bend low to pick up any
potatoes that fall off the wagon. Their arms golden with dust.
Their hair matted, shimmering in the sun. All week long, in the
late afternoon heat, wagons filled with potatoes. Now we will bag
those potatoes, now the brand-new paper bags wait for our hands.
 The ground trembles and buzzes, the energy of the black
conveyor line building up speed, quickly flowing forward. Negro
shovels potatoes from the back of the wagon onto the conveyor,
the pitchfork twanging from potatoes bouncing and falling
against its steel prongs. Changó stands on the side of the line, in
the middle of the potatoes nudging against each other like fish
fighting their way upstream, watching for bad potatoes, clumps
of soil, weeds, rocks—he pulls, up come the long roots of a rogue
soybean plant. Arturo and Boogaloo wait at the end of the line,
the potatoes schooling up against each other. They dip their
hands down like nets, scooping up potatoes. They drop them into
scales until they have ten pounds, then tip the scales, dropping
the potatoes into empty bags. In unison, each sweeps a bag onto a
waist-high table and turns back to start again. Tino twists copper
bands around the tops of the bags, lifts one off the table, swinging the bag in flight to me, and I catch it and stack the ten-pound
bag on a pallet, the first pallet in a long line that I will stack in
a five-by-three design, alternating the pattern every layer, until
the pallets are six rows high. Once a bag is set into the pattern,
I must turn, for Tino will throw another and I must catch it and
lay it down and keep going, catch stack turn catch, the pattern
becoming part of my hands, arms, part of my muscles, stacking
catching turning, part of my blood, the rhythm pumping through
me, creating the intimacy of this paper, these copper bands, my
sweat, the roundness of the potatoes against the palms of my
hands. The motion turning, circling—I must keep going, my
hands sore, must keep stacking and turning and catching faster.
 Hurry up, hijo, Boogaloo sings.

> You don't have a row straight
> Your hands bricks
> Feet stones
> Bones like sticks
> Are ready to break
> Ready to escape
> Are ready to run away

A bag falls from my hands, hits the ground. I bend over. Tino grunts. A bag strikes my back, the copper band digging into my shoulder blade. I turn. Another bag knocks my hand against the pallet.

You are falling behind, hijo.

Tu vida es muy lenta
y la del viejo es rápida

Boogaloo won't stop. He's singing, dropping full scales into bags in a fast rhythm to match his hard words.

I kick the fallen bags away, turn back and try to find my rhythm. Inside, I try to block out Boogaloo's words with my own song, with a rhythm that could drown out his laughter. If only I could sing out, Fuck you—you black Boogaloo—Boogaloo, you black fuck—I don't know you and you aren't anything to me and is that your face smiling or your ass? *Es la cara? O es el culo?*

I want to sing so Boogaloo will remember that I walked up and asked about the Help Wanted sign, while he and my father and the rest of the men sat in the car and passed around a bottle of Don Q. *Yes, you can work here, son. Bring your father and your friends—bring as many as you can. We pay $3.50 an hour, but you can go over to Berrien Center and apply for food stamps. And you can live out back.*

I turn, catch a bag, place it down. Inside the market, people buy fruits and vegetables. I stood in front of a table of asparagus and listened to Mr. Vollman. I listened and looked out through the back door, out across the strawberry patches and potato fields, seeing the white cabin we would move into. A shack, no bigger than a child's bedroom: a leaning square of wood with a table in the corner, a propane burner on top, a single bulb hanging from the ceiling, two dusty mattresses lying on the floor. Boogaloo sleeps every night—a broad smile, his eyelids fluttering—like he's dreaming of the most beautiful and happiest of worlds, and he never recognizes that I stood there and listened to Mr. Vollman's words. Piles of freshly picked asparagus glistened on the table, customers lifting bunches into plastic bags. I felt their eyes, heard their words—*Look at that boy. Look at how dirty he is.*

It wasn't you, Boogaloo.

I listened, looked down at the concrete floor, my hands balled up inside my pants pockets. I stood there for my father.

My song goes unheard, wouldn't matter to Boogaloo. I catch bags, try to keep up, set them down, try to make the pattern of my life hold together. Catch a bag, lay it down. The scales echo, vibrate against the rafters. Sparrows fly and sing, swerving in and out of the barn, their curved shadows fluttering across the dirt floor. The conveyor belt rumbles on. The pitchfork twanging, the sound reverberating down the line against the back of my skull. I lay a bag down.

Outside, cars glide down US 31 in a steady stream of color and chrome, pulling in and out of the gravel lot, customers shuffling in out of the market, dust lifting in a swirl, their arms full with brimming bags and baskets of plums, apricots, apples, peaches, sweet corn. A girl walks across the lot. Her long black hair tied with a yellow ribbon. Dressed in a pair of cut-offs, her tanned legs flexing underneath a light sheen of sun-colored down. She has on a white bikini top with pineapples scattered about. She gracefully pulls her legs into the backseat of her station wagon. Her father hands her a basket of plums, closes her door, and he and her mother get in and drive away. To let go. Lay a bag down: to let go: to be free like them.

Tino throws me another bag. The bags are clean, white, the paper smooth and soft against my hands, printed with the silhouette of some red mountains, a green stream running in between them. The dusty smell sweet and light inside the pole barn, the sun beating down hot on the tin roof. I lay the bag down. I turn, wait. Tino pushing on the back of his hips, stretching his spine. Negro's smiling, bent over, beads of sweat raining from his black face onto the stream of potatoes, his muscles in knots, the pitchfork standing in the midst of the potatoes. He points to Boogaloo.

Almost done, hijo. You've worked hard, Ernestito.

Boogaloo's face twists into a smile, a grimace of sweat. He lets out a deep sigh, his breath whistling through his teeth as if he's been talking for a while.

Tino throws me another bag, then the last one. I lift up the bags I dropped, lay them on the pallet. Changó takes his box of rocks and clumps of dirt to the rock pile out back. Arturo walks over, turns off the power. The lights flicker. The conveyor belt dies with a final surge of electricity evaporating into the dark corners of the barn.

Here you go, Ernie. Mr. Vollman hands me my check along with my father's.

Boogaloo comes trotting up, wiping his back and underarms with his shirt. Arturo follows behind laughing. Negro jumps off the wagon, runs forward. Tino rubs the dust from his pants, slowly approaches.

Mr. Vollman turns to them.

Okay, that's all. *Nada ma,* he announces, wiping the sweat from his forehead as if he has worked alongside us, as if he feels the rawness of my inner thighs, the chapped, tender skin of my hands. As though he feels the tiredness of the summer's heat and sweat from driving up and down the lanes to drop us off and pick us up.

Boogaloo steps in front of Mr. Vollman, tucks his check into his pants, then shows him how to shake the solidarity way: first, a regular handshake; followed by a thumb grip; then a hard shake with a knuckle grip; finally to let go and hit each other's closed fists.

Mr. Vollman chuckles, his head turned up, his lips raised high over his teeth.

Boogaloo smiles, the red sunburnt arm of Mr. Vollman grazing his arm.

For a moment, I see Mr. Vollman as decent and caring, a man no different than any of us. He has a wife, two young daughters. One Sunday afternoon I walked up the hill to Mr. Vollman's farmhouse to tell him we had run out of propane. He stood out in the yard, underneath a big oak tree, pushing his daughters on a tire swing. On a picnic table in neat little rows, sparkling in the sun, Mrs. Vollman had canning jars filled with fruits and vegetables, jams and jellies. She came out in her apron and gave me a loaf of bread she had baked and a jar of blueberry jam. Mr. Vollman never looked at me. He stopped swinging his girls, looked out across his fields, and told me we could build a fire in the yard, and tomorrow he'd have some propane delivered. I walked away, down the hill, the bread warm under my arm, not wanting to hate Mr. Vollman but knowing throughout my life I may have no choice but to work for people like him, and they would take advantage of me, they would pay me what they pleased, they could always send me off to a tired shack out back.

At the bottom of the hill, on the edge of a potato field, I sat down in a clump of raspberry bushes. I heard the girls laughing. I opened the jar of jam. In the distance a dog barked, and out on the highway I could hear trucks and cars. I ate the whole jar of jam with my fingers, the berries sweet and soft in my mouth, the tips of my fingers blue. The girls laughed again, their voices happy and shrill. I looked up the hill. Mr. Vollman pushed them on their swing, his white shirt rolled to his elbows, a smile on his face, the cool air rushing through the girls' long blond hair. I tried to get up and leave, but their voices, my sour stomach, some

74

birds thrashing in the bushes—they all made me cry. And then I retched under the bushes and buried the jar deep within them. I walked back to the shack, my throat dry and sore, the loaf of bread tucked under my arm for my father and the men.

Changó walks back into the pole barn carrying his box. He sets it underneath the conveyor belt, pulls out his shirttails, wipes his face—brown handprints and wide sweeps of dirt smudging his shirt. He's exhausted, his face drenched with streams of dirty sweat, sick from too much drink, his cheeks saggy, his lips purple and thin. He pulls out a comb, slicks back his hair. My father still wears the same white dress shirts and black pants he wore when my mother lived at home. In the evening, after our dinner, I walk down to the stream that runs out back of our shack, and I wash my father's shirts the best I can with a bar of soap, by beating them against the rocks.

Changó pats the top of his hair, slides his comb into his back pocket.

Keeping my father's shirts clean seems to keep him alive, seems to give us both a piece of my mother.

We all head away from the market and the pole barn, out past the old strawberry patches of June, the plants wilted and smashed down to a phlegm-colored yellow by the sun, and across the breadth of the patch, dried husks and stalks of sweet corn lie scattered and torn. Negro and Arturo are a good ways ahead, headed out toward the potato fields, heat-mirages fluttering behind their dust-caked boots. Tino stops to the right, at the trash heap. He lifts a red mesh bag of onions. Taking his short, blunt knife from his waistband, he stabs through the top of the bag; the bag rips open like a fresh wound, onions bleeding out onto the dust in a thud. He kicks a few of the onions over with the tips of his shoes, looking for what's salvageable, then bends down, stabs an onion, lifts it up, bends down again, stabs another. Cutting away at the soft, black outer edges, he slips the onion hearts into the front left pocket of his pants. My father comes from behind with the jagged end of a watermelon; its insides hang out—fleshy, red, wet, raw. Boogaloo drinks from a carton of orange juice, spits it back out, a long stream of foamy orange and white, a gush of acid and mold filling the air.

I step to the trash. Raising a broken fruit crate, I lift a head of lettuce that doesn't look half bad.

Ah, lechuga para el conejo, Boogaloo hisses.

Changó laughs.

His eyes red, rheumy, and watery in the midday sun, Tino wipes his knife against the front of his dust-covered blue pants.

Yes, Boogaloo, and this rabbit has worked quick and light today, Tino says in my defense.

Pero viejo, no matter how quick the rabbit, it's always caught and skinned, Boogaloo counters.

Tino holds the handle of his knife, stares at Boogaloo.

He laughs, his white teeth sparkling in the sun. And then, to spite Tino, Boogaloo jabs:

Y viejo, no matter how old the goat, it will still make good stew.

My father cackles, shuffles down the lane in a cloud of dust, the injured watermelon raised over his shoulder dripping seeds and juice into his footprints.

Tino doesn't say a word. He looks at Boogaloo for a moment, then me, rubbing the handle of his knife. He heads up the lane, following Changó. Boogaloo walks away, following behind Tino and singing:

> *Conejo y cabra*
> *La sopa de mi vida*
> *El viejo y el hijo*
> *Los dos camachos*
> *Elegantes como burros*
> *Conejo y cabra*
> *La sopa de mi vida*
> *Cabra y conejo*

The song rises, stabs loud into my chest as I walk behind them to the shack following red footprints.

Arturo is filling a pan with water from the irrigation sprinkler. Negro washes off some potatoes he has dug from the field. Tino hands Negro the onion hearts to wash off, takes the pan from Arturo to put on the propane burner inside. Under the black walnut tree in front of the shack, I pull out the jar of mayonnaise and the salt and pepper shakers we have shaded with newspaper inside a cardboard box.

Tráeme la botella, Changó yells.

The engine in Boogaloo's passion-purple Plymouth fires up. I turn back, the engine revs, then idles with the sweet sound of salsa escaping out of the car's windows. The metallic silver-flecked Duster glitters in the late afternoon light. The chrome mag wheels, the scrubbed jet-black tires, silver splashing across the grass. The Duster's jacked up, with yellow traction bars hanging behind the tires. On the side windows, decals of the roadrunner and the words *Meep-Meep*, two lime-green palm trees outlined in neon orange framing the cursive *Local Motion*.

This is a car, a silver dream. A father buys it for his son, fills up the gas tank, gives him a twenty so he can go out. Cruising up and down Main Street, his two friends by his side, they take US 31 out to Thomas Stadium, the Hayloft Ice Cream Parlor. All the girls sitting on the hoods of their cars in shorts, white blouses, sundresses, their summer-tanned bodies glowing in the cool night air, licking cold, soft ice cream cones.

A sweet, *cherry* car is what Boogaloo says he always wanted. He told me how with the money he saved from working at the Star-Kist tuna factory in Mayagüez, he flew to Miami and bought this Duster at the first classic car lot he found. All those dreams, all his work, only to drive back to Niles, only to return and work in these fields. He never drives the car. He washes and waxes it. He starts it to charge the battery. He turns the stereo loud to hear his songs. But Boogaloo never drives it. We work all day and, no matter how tired we are, no matter how late it is once we get cleaned up, we still walk to the bar. We work all week and don't do anything on Sunday but sit under the shade of the walnut tree as Boogaloo puts on a one-man show of his favorite *jíbaro* tales and guarachas. Sometimes I want to tell him I'm tired of his tales, his songs, tired of how easy it is for him to conjure up some memory from when he was little, some evening when he saw a man dancing in the street, some little snatch of song or joke he overheard on some lazy afternoon and has so easily taken within himself and turned into a moment of significance, my father and the other men sitting under the tree mesmerized by his words. I want to tell him to take us away, that he should drive us to Lake Michigan, just drive us away from these fields.

I remember my father's cars: a 1966 Impala, a convertible Camaro, a yellow Mustang, the wind on my face, a neck scarf ruffling aside my mother's hair, my father driving along the sea.

Aye, que suave, Arturo sings, shaking his hips to the beat by the irrigation sprinkler.

Everyone gathers by the edge of the tree, inside the circle of shade. I pass the bottle around. I drink last. The rum's thick, hot, bristly in the pocket of my stomach; then it evens out, feels like smooth waves rolling against a shore, churning out cool from my skin. I hand the bottle to my father, walk out to the back of the shack to take a piss.

Boogaloo begins to sing:

Que me duele la cabeza
Tráeme una cerveza
Que me duele el corazón
Tráeme un palo de ron

I look back to his voice. Negro strips off his shirt and pants, jumps into the sprinkler.

Arturo yells out: *Dame el jabón.*

The engine revs to a high whine, shuts off. I walk away, underneath the clothesline suspended between a small pine tree and the corner of the shack, the line straining with soiled boxer shorts, black socks, white V-neck undershirts, the men's clean *guayaberas* for tonight's drinking. The rum churns through my body in a deep rhythmic wave, splashing against the tips of my fingers and toes, only to crash and begin the revolution of beating water telling me: Ernest, *Ernestito,* you're starting to feel okay, it'll be okay for you'll drink more, and all your tiredness will go away. I pee on a cracked-in-half cinder block, my pee splashing onto the dust, the sound of so much water rushing back across my hair, through my ears. I listen to the strength of this voice, feel those banal words, *it'll be okay,* hear the way my mother always whispered what she thought of as a touch of grace.

The sun begins to fall toward the northwest horizon of Lake Michigan. Soon night will come, there will be more laughter, more drink. I can hear my father and Tino talking inside the shack. Negro lets out a howl, Arturo giggling. I zip my pants, turn, walk back toward the voices.

They're all in hysterics. Boogaloo is standing out in the field scrubbing his Afro with a bar of soap. Arturo guides the water from the irrigation sprinkler toward his naked body, hard streams of water hitting Boogaloo's thighs, his chest. For a moment, it is as if I have stepped into a small, undiscovered moment: Boogaloo's broad-white-smile; his wrinkled eyes tightly shut; rivulets of foaming soap suds flowing over his bulging biceps, coursing down his sleek body; his skin shiny under the water like a piece of hardwood; his stiff penis knifing across the water-shrouded air, as he moves his body in the rhythm of his hard scrubbing.

Boogaloo *is* human. He laughs, his teeth gnash, he turns, bends, shaking his ass at Arturo, flapping his arms. I step

forward, seeing Boogaloo for real, as if he might have once been
a boy living in a small white house with a nice green yard. His
father turning on the sprinkler on a humid day. Boogaloo running
through the arcing water, a rainbow of colors flowing onto the
grass, turning into the most beautiful of greens in the world.

What you looking at, pichichi? *¿Qué, tu quieres mis huevos?*
Boogaloo yells, grabbing his balls.

Arturo and Negro turn, staring at me. They laugh. Prance
on the grass and dance in the circle of water. Arturo runs to
Boogaloo and grabs his ass. Negro yelps, runs, and then slides
face first, his arms skidding water against my legs. He stands,
runs again and slides. Arturo and Boogaloo wrestle in the arc of
the irrigation sprinkler.

The shack door slams open. Tino walks out waving his knife
in the air, muttering *pendejos y cabrones*, a pan of cooked potatoes
steaming in his other hand, a wooden spoon sticking out of the
top. Changó follows behind, Tino stepping underneath the tree.
The men stop playing, look at him, the sound of water sprinkling
the ground. They smell the food and begin to dry off and dress.

Tino calls to Arturo to bring over a piece of tin. On top of
a cinder block, Arturo sets the piece of tin. Tino flatly places the
pot on top. Changó adds salt and pepper, then mayonnaise. Negro
comes over with the onion hearts. Tino chops them up in the
curve of his palm. I bring the head of lettuce, ripping shreds that
fall into the pot. Tino begins to mix it all up—

Párate, viejo, Boogaloo yells, shaking on one pant leg at a
time. He clasps his belt. He walks over and pulls out two little
green peppers, and a bigger pepper that's mostly red with a hint
of green.

Back home, my mother boils the skin of a pineapple, mixing
the juice with garlic, black pepper and salt, and a few peppers.

Boogaloo holds out his hand in the circle of men. He looks
into my eyes.

She put it all inside a rum bottle and set it in the sun.

He closes his hand, shakes his fist up at the evening sun.

She told me: *Cómelo con fuerza*. Then she sprinkled it on my
food.

Boogaloo shakes his hand over the pot, his eyes closed, then
looks into my eyes again.

You'll never be afraid of hell, she told me.

All the men nod in agreement.

My father stirs the pot quickly, sets the spoon down. He says,
Yes. Mine the same. Ernest . . . remember when abuela made

some, those bottles hanging from her front porch with white string . . .

His voice trails off. He lifts the spoon, then drops it. He takes a drink of rum, his face white, his lips quivering. He looks at me but he can't speak, his eyes blank, my father lost within his memory of fields.

Tino rubs my father's shoulder, pats him on the back.

Boogaloo reaches toward the pot, handing Tino the peppers—he stops. He looks into the sky, around the circle, deep into the fields. There's pure silence save the irrigation sprinkler stiffly splashing the fields. Boogaloo seems to strain his ears as if there's someone here who shouldn't be. Everyone concentrates. Listens intently to what may come next out of Boogaloo's half-smiling face.

Todo somos hombres aquí. Pero el hijo, you, my little one, who works like a rabbit—you, Ernestito, must tell us if these peppers *pican.*

He offers me the peppers. I quickly raise a green pepper to my mouth and bite it in half, chew it up and swallow.

From underneath the shade of the tree, inside the circle of these men, I can no longer tell if there is an evening sun, if night has suddenly arrived. All the men look at me. Their heads look bigger, like they're wearing masks: Negro's blank, black-as-tar stare; Arturo's leather-colored grimace; Tino's red, watery, beat-up eyes; Boogaloo's broad-white-mocking-smile, his face telling me: *Oh, I feel sorry for you—oh, hijo, you're a disgrace—you'll always play the fool.*

My father lets out a louder whimper. His eyes bloodshot, his eyelids fluttering up and down heavily. Small tears roll down his cheeks, a noise coming from his mouth like he's choking. He holds the rum bottle by the neck, shifts up on his knees, and swings hard at Boogaloo's head. Boogaloo jerks back, holds up his fists, sticks out his long pink tongue, then laughs, his head swinging back and forth.

No, no, no, Tino yells, pushing my father back off his knees. He holds my father's arm, takes away the bottle.

It's okay, Changó, take it easy.

Boogaloo's head dances from behind his raised fists, his tongue licking the air; Arturo and Negro laughing.

My throat burns, my tongue on fire, my lips swelling, ears ringing with the beating heat rising in my head. The laughter turning louder, echoing from the circle of men, rising into the branches of the tree. Tino turns from my father and hands me a potato peel. I chew on it, pressing the wet skin against my tongue. He hands me the rum, and I let it fill my mouth, swish it around, hold it underneath my tongue and along my cheeks, and then swallow. I stand, yelling, cursing inside myself. Even though my father was angry, he now smiles and giggles, waving for me to hand him the bottle. I hand him the rum, and he takes a long drink. His hand shakes, his cheeks flushed, his eyes closed. My fists clench and I curse him for having me in this field, for letting me work amongst these men who roll on their backs and laugh, and I curse myself for having the hope that I could hold our lives together, that one day everything would be okay.

I walk away from their laughter, away from their voices, out toward the back of the shack. The wind rustles the pines. The scent of manure, wet rocks, and pine. The fields, the orchards shaded with deep blues and purples in the evening heat. In the distance, on the northwest horizon, the sun barely visible, dropping into a line of cottonwoods. I walk toward the sea of fields that lie in front of me, my lips swollen, my throat dry, my inner thighs chafing with each stride. Faster and faster, my hot senses arcing in front of me, I walk toward the horizon, the purpling air hanging like spiderwebs connecting all the trees in the orchard. Following a low path into a patch of red raspberries, I splash through the puddles mirroring their bumpy undersides, the water cool across my face.

August. In this heat, after this day, after this past year, it is easy for me to see that I will never be unreliable; there is just too much truth. I can't come up with some story, some song, like Boogaloo or my father. I can't escape my life through dreams.

Last August, on a ninety-degree day, my mother left my father. He was sitting under a tree, on a wooden apple crate, and I with him, in the shade, stayed behind. We lost the house we rented; during the winter, on Main Street, we lived in the Four Flags Hotel; this summer we came to work in these fields. A simple gesture: I stayed behind. There is no story, there is no music, there is no song. There is only the day-to-day living inside my skin.

I step onto a stone road, a northwest breeze cool against my bare arms. I can walk west, cross the river, follow a path around the edge of a cranberry bog, and soon I'll reach the shores of Lake Michigan. I can leave my father and his circle of men behind: I can move into my own world, move out into my own fate. No longer will I have to think of Boogaloo, a mean man who does not care that I only want to be a fifteen-year-old boy with a home. And, away from Boogaloo and the men, I will no longer blame my father, I will only see him for who he is: the man who I always hoped would find some happiness, who I tried to help escape from the deep music of work and pain he was born into.

A loud roar, the dusty road kicking up stones and dirt. A mirage of purple and silver, swimming in waves of dust. Boogaloo glides his Duster onto the side of the road. He and Tino emerge, sharp, elegant in their white guayaberas.

I walk toward them.

Boogaloo hands me a cigarette.

Escúchame, hijo. Don't be mad.

Tino hands me a bottle.

I look at both of them so clean and shiny in the middle of the dusty road. Nobody speaks. The leaves on the cottonwoods rustle together. I take a long drink.

First the conga drums, the starting rhythm, the *cuatro* guitars strumming the melody, the güiro scratching out a two-count, then the maracas rattling from the car to echo upon the stone road. A jíbaro guaracha escaping from the car.

Tino closes his eyes, taps his hands on his thigh, sways loosely, free like a mango tree shaking in the breeze.

Ay—oh—mami—oh. God bless you. *Mami,* God bless you, come the screams from the backseat. We all turn. Changó lifts a bottle, the rum gurgles into his lips tightly wrapped around the end. His head tipped back, his eyes closed. He looks to be in a dream: his black hair slicked back off his forehead, his head falling against the backseat, his silky brown arms next to his light-blue guayabera. His face white like bones, except for the tears running down his flushed cheeks.

I turn to give Boogaloo his cigarette.

With his arm around my shoulder, he says in a quivering voice:

Ernest, no, hombre. You keep it.

Tino drops his head, walks back to the car, opens the door, lifts up the front seat.

There's no more hope in the backseat. There's only my father's weak, crying body, and, with no hope left, only for the love of my father do I enter into the backseat where the guaracha beats strong, only for love do I sit down and let the song engulf me.

FACING NORTH, FACING SOUTH

There is always a knife in his stories, a rose, the bloom of blood—
or, at least, a bruise. Purple ribs of pain are where I find my
father: that eternal story of his own father forcing him to quit
school in the third grade so he could work in the fields, the silver
of a machete glinting in the air, the flat of the blade striking his
back, driving him down the red dirt road. A legend crookedly
layered within the furrows of my regret and shame: the luxury
of splashing cool clean water on my face in the morning, the lost
moments following the pulsing throats of hummingbirds, the
soft, unworked shape of my hands turning blue and white and
cold in certain weathers (seasonal emotional geographical). Those
moments—at dinner, in a meeting, after I've *pffd* breath through
my teeth, grunted, or smiled the smile of smiles—moments when
someone suddenly believes I am foreign, some dark man they've
witnessed running through a terminal, focused on the threadbare
elbows of his coat, catching the musty smell of cheap rum mixed
with days of travel as he grips a cardboard valise too tightly.
    Always this migration to hands, these two thick books I carry at
my sides, my palms written in a script I am still trying to memorize.
    My father. Here he is in this photograph, turned to the bone-
white light of the moon falling through the window, now
arranged alongside others, and then for a moment I make out the
outline of my father's working childhood: the sharp sweat in his
eyes, the cutting burn of a rope along his wrist, his heart har-
vested by those ripening seasons of pineapples, mangoes, cane.
The bright blood of guavas. A worn passage of time in a red rut-
ted path of dust the ox leaves behind. That tired season of work
so deep that when the heavy rains fall, water fills the path and
laps the ox's sweaty and gray belly. For a moment, in each of his
steps, the water swirls carmine. Tonight, I smell almonds floating
in the sea, turn the hourglass over in a circle of moonlight, face
the sands slowly outlining a death mask.

EXILE'S HOME

When he woke it was to the smell of almonds floating in the sea. His father had laid him on the outer wall of el Morro, his suit coat folded under his head, a round stone pressing into the small of his back. At first, the *mango piragua* his father had bought him was sweet and cold in the deep pocket of his stomach, then the sun rose higher, and Ernest's head was suddenly drenched with cool sweat, and once again, as had happened often in the last few weeks, Ernest fell to his knees, the insides of his arms pressed hard against his ribs, his stomach letting go: an orange gush of liquid streaming from his mouth. Now his father took his wet handkerchief and wiped Ernest's hands. He felt his father move away, yellow heat penetrating the darkness of his eyelids. He opened his eyes: the bright blue sky, a few puffy clouds. The light didn't hurt anymore, and he could feel his hair drying from the breeze.

Changó lifted his head and slid underneath him, resting Ernest's head on his lap.

Out across the bay billowing fumes rose from gray smokestacks, and down below Ernest saw tightly built houses with thin tin roofs, their water urns and troughs lined with silver and blue, clotheslines connecting each house with flags of red and green, black and white, a flutter of cloth in the breeze. A balding dog ran down an alleyway, its bits of white fur matted and mottled with pink, chasing a little boy running with a stick, clouds of red dust dancing between them.

Changó raised Ernest's head and slid from underneath him. He lifted Ernest to his feet. He held Ernest around the waist, pointing with his other arm across the bay.

The Bacardi plant.

He released Ernest, stood below the wall in front of him. He pulled Ernest closer and embraced him. He whispered: You be okay, Ernestito. Don't be sad.

Ernest looked at his father, but he had his face turned down. The breeze surged above the wall, deafening his ears, and he caught the scent of sugar cane boiling. When the breeze stopped, he heard, Maybe one day we come back.

Changó wiped his face with the back of his hand, then quickly turned to Ernest. He tucked Ernest's shirt back in, tucking all the front wrinkles deep into his pants. He loosened Ernest's tie and pulled it from around his neck. Carefully, he folded the tie in a square, tucking it inside the breast pocket of his suit coat. He lifted Ernest down from the wall. He took out his comb, softly combing back Ernest's hair.

Look, Ernest said, pointing out across the bay, out off the island to the deeper sea.

A bank of silver clouds seemed to cut the blue sky in half, and the sea below was no longer blue but turned black. The sea's surface shook, and Ernest could see silver curtains of rain swaying and falling from the clouds. Ernest thought of how wet and cool the sea must be out there, the sea itself wet with rain.

Ernest lifted his father's hand and softly kissed his palm.

His father let go of his hand. There were no sounds, only small tears softly running down his brown cheeks, catching, then falling from his father's chin.

Ernest wanted to tell him, *Maybe one day you'll come back.* Changó didn't look sad or angry; he had a far-off, frightened look in his eyes. He thought his father seemed unsure, perhaps afraid because they were going to Michigan, because he would see Ernest's mother for the first time in nine months.

His father wiped his eyes. He gently rubbed Ernest's cheek with his thumb, his tears warm on his face. He took him by the waist, lifting him onto the wall.

You so skinny. Your mom won't know you.

Changó laughed for a moment, then his voice caught with phlegm. He spit.

One day, Ernest, you might do something and not know.

Changó opened his mouth, as if out of breath, then shut it. He looked at Ernest and said, But I will take you home.

He pulled from his suit pocket a small, dark-green bundle tied with white string. He gave the bundle to Ernest, turned away, and walked to the edge of the parapet. He looked out on the sea.

Ernest lightly squeezed the strange bundle, a banana leaf folded around something square. He untied the small piece of string, the corners of the leaf curling up, Ernest smelling rain, dirt, and the leafy green of plantains. There were immaculate white envelopes inside, the cotton paper soft to the touch. There was no writing on them. He turned them over, the flaps sealed with a thick green wax, and imprinted in the wax a chubby little bear hugging a pot of honey. His mother—she had sent these envelopes, she had let him sit curled in her lap, his head inside the curve of her arm, laying his head on her chest, the book held out in front of them. He may have only been three or four, but he remembered her, remembered her hennaed hair scintillating the light, the sweet smell of her powdered neck. She would cover the illustrations with her right hand, carefully reading the words,

> So for a week Christopher Robin read that sort of
> book at the North end of Pooh, and Rabbit hung
> his washing on the South end . . . and in between
> Bear felt himself getting slenderer and slenderer.
> And at the end of the week Christopher Robin
> said, "Now!"

The words always came first. His mother wanted him to hear the words, their sounds, to come to know things through their sounds before he ever saw them.

He closed his eyes listening to her hearing her heartbeat feeling her warm breath smelling hearing her words.

> How he dreamed to be a cloud
> Floating above the sea
> For a moment
> A little cloud
> Singing aloud in shades of blue

His thumb grazed over the ridges of the miniature honey jar. His father leaned back against the wall, smoking a cigarette, little clouds of white covering his face, surrounded by the blue of the sky, the blue of the sea. He threw his cigarette over the parapet. He looked at Ernest, dropped his head, his hands shaking at his sides.

Ernest laid the banana leaf flat on the wall. He placed the envelopes down, and began to fold the leaf up. He stopped. He took one envelope and broke its seal. He unfolded the letter.

15, December
Dear Ernest,
    Today I found a small volume, just the right size

*for your coat pocket, filled with illustrations of ships
and boats, and wonderful stories of seas and rivers,
long journeys. And I ran into an old friend, Ramóna
and her daughter. . .*

For now it was enough. He saw her handwriting, the elegant,
elongated, thin black ink, the way she had taught him to write
his *E* with an upside-down seven, a line through the middle and
around the top, thus the sound of the vowel stretching into the
breath of his name—*Ernest.* He heard *sea, journey.* There were
small dots of purple ink on the paper, and he could see her holding her pen above the page, her face stilled in contemplation,
her hair shiny in a shaft of light. He quickly put the letter away,
pressing the wax seal with his thumb. He folded the corners of
the banana leaf, then tied it with the white string. He lifted his
suit coat from the wall, found his right pocket, and slid the bundle
inside. He slipped his coat on. He lifted his father's handkerchief
from the wall.

Ernest unfurled the handkerchief, letting the sea breeze rush
through it. He folded it in half, then doubled the fold. He tried to
then turn each corner into the center. Before he left the mainland
nine months ago, Ernest's mother had made for him a man's rose
from his handkerchief. He couldn't get the shape exactly the same
as his mother had, but when he looked up into his father's face
he knew he understood. His father bent over. Ernest tucked the
man's rose into his father's breast pocket.

His father put his arm around Ernest's shoulder. Ernest
slipped his arm around his waist. With his head against his
father's side, he could hear his heartbeat, feel the lightness of his
father, sense he was calm to have him by his side. Ernest felt his
own side—the bundle of letters thick in his pocket. He knew his
father hadn't opened or read any of them, because the wax seals
had not been broken, and because his father couldn't read, because
whatever letter they arrived within, his father would've had to
have had someone read it to him—and, his father knew that these
letters, with their little waxed bears, these were for Ernest.

His father squeezed him harder, humming a soft song.

A boat let out a deep, long whistle. Docked down below, in
the small cove next to the tightly built tin-roofed houses, the
boat billowed black smoke, idling. The engine died, and when the
smoke disappeared, Ernest saw the boy who had been chased by
the little bald dog: now he ran down the lane, the dog beside him,
his stick turning a rusty bicycle wheel, clouds of dust lifting from

his feet. He hit the wheel one last time, the wheel spinning onto the sand, the dog trying to catch it, a froth of waves knocking the wheel down, the dog jumping back with a yelp from the sea. The boy ran across the sand to the pier, then jumped down into the boat. Swiftly, he reappeared, a fat burlap sack over his shoulders, his dark muscular legs struggling under the weight. He carried the load down the pier—men passing him quickly with two or three bags hoisted on their shoulders—and dropped the bag on a cart waiting at the end. He ran back to the boat, this time appearing with a long bundle of green bananas.

Ernest let go of his father's waist. His father raised Ernest's hand and kissed his palm. Ernest held his father's hand, looking at the many thin cuts and jagged lines, the thick pink scar on the edge of his wrist from a machete. He remembered all the stories he had heard of his father being forced to quit school in the third grade to work in the fields. In these cuts and lines, in the warmth of his hand, in the clarity of the sky, in the blue of the sea, the waves rising and falling, surging *caracol* after *caracol*, Ernest surged with his father's story, with his memory of fields.

A gust blew through his hair, the sea turning deep green, silver, back to blue and full of sun.

Once, on the edge of a cane field, there was a white ox chained to a mill, always walking in a circle, walking so much that rain filled its path, its gray-white belly wet with sweat and rain, Ernest feeling in his mind the rippling muscles of the ox when Changó ran his hand along his stomach. Changó would then hug his arms, say how they burned from unloading the carts stacked with cane.

The boat whistled. The cart of goods turned up the lane, pulled by a team of oxen, the little bald dog yapping at the side of the teamster. The young boy stood next to the sea, the bicycle wheel against one leg, the stick against the other, drinking deeply from an orange soda, his arms and face glistening with sweat, powdered with red dust.

Ernest suddenly felt better than he had in the last two weeks, his stomach hard, his insides filled with sudden urgency, a place close to his heart pounding with the weight of his mother's letters.

He squeezed his father's hand, twice.

Changó, let's go. We can't miss our plane.

For Pablo Medina

AVENUE OF THE AMERICAS, CIRCA 1952

Standing against a wall, an immaculate white cloth draped over
a tray, Changó, nine years old, stands military straight, a jagged
straw hat cocked on his head, a tattered shirt smudged with dirt
reaching just below his elbows. Coloring the pristine white cloth,
three green and red mangoes, a pair of cow shanks and hooves, a
pig's foot, a chopped-up ox tail, the translucent bones clean and
vivid with blood, with the succulent morsels found there. These
butcher scraps, this respite from his sore hands in a field holding
a machete. This white cloth dazzling against his dirty clothes,
his eyes. Changó must've washed it each night in a clear running
stream he heard singing of shells and stars on its shapely voyage
to the sea.

People pass, anticipating the briefest gestures of a hand in
a pocket, the click of a gold clasp on a purse, he's ready for this
woman who stops to buy a piece for stew. A few coins shimmer
on the cloth next to a pale goat's tongue.

For a moment, beyond his memory of fields—picking thorny
pineapples outside Arecibo, harvesting coffee in the mountains of
Lares, cutting cane in the low fields of Añasco, selling mangoes
in a plaza in the dusk—my father follows the blue cobblestones
of the avenue, catches the fading sunlight still bright on the
facade of a lime green house. Within the undulating grillwork
of a black balcony, in those delicately rendered cast-iron vines of
roses and leaves, seashells and stars, he gazes from within himself at a young boy who sees without the sting of sweat in his
eyes.

WESTERN AVENUE

From the distance, the blinking lights of the ethanol plant's blue
smokestacks. In this November light the freshly turned fields
glisten coal black, a few cornstalks still standing, their thin leaves
rustling in the wind. In the summers the sweet smell of the surrounding mint fields. Now the stench of the refining ethanol
holding close to the ground. The heavy odor—something like
burnt baked potatoes, fried chicken, mixing with smoldering
vinyl. On the other side of the refinery, Vulcan's air-compressors
suck and hiss, and the material lines thump the resin powder
from the outside silos. The factory in full production. Men standing at the end of a line, inside the throttled pitch of the slam-
ming punches, the concrete floor quaking with each downward
punch. Saws whirring across panels, vinyl snowing into the air
and powdering the floor. The wind blowing off Lake Michigan at
five below. Their arms turning, inside this heat of one hundred
degrees. They turn their arms and flip the twelve-foot pieces of
vinyl siding into a box. Every three and a half minutes, they fill a
box with twenty-one panels.

Two men stand at the opposite end of a packing table. They
bend over, slam the box lid down, beating their fists against its
glued lips, then staple each end with an air-powered staple gun.
One of the men pushes down a lever, the packing table opening,
and they turn the box on its side and lift and swing the box from
the table to a pallet on a wagon.

A forklift backs up. The driver jumps down. He lifts the
wagon's tongue to the forklift's hitch, and jams in place the steel
pin. He takes off his gloves, lays them on the seat, pulls out a
cigarette. He leans against the forklift, smoking and watching the
men turn a box on its side, turning their arms to take hold and
lift and throw the box onto the wagon. In three and a half minutes they'd have the last box, and then he'd pull away another full
load.

Ernest walked along his and Danilo's lines. The red emergency lights blinked crazily on top of his extruder's control panel. Four years into this new life as an extruder operator, and these lights still caused his stomach to drop, adrenaline and worry pounding through his arms. His foreman, Dave, was up on the catwalk. He beat on the material lines with a steel bar. Danilo, Ernest's line partner, walked forward. He rubbed his eyes and yawned.

You on break, Danilo, or me?

Ah, Ernesto, I tired. No sleep today, Danilo answered.

Ernest and Danilo had been hired at Vulcan's on the same day—Ernest in the morning, Danilo in the afternoon, six weeks after he gained an exit visa from Poland—and they always worked the twelve-hour night shift and chose adjoining lines. They had a system; one would watch the lines while the other took a long break.

You check the hopper, Danilo?

He shrugged, picked up a wrench. They could hear Dave beating on the lines. Over the speaker system someone called for a maintenance man to check the material hopper down on line number three.

Ernest liked working with Danilo. They lived in the same Polish neighborhood in South Bend and took turns driving to work. Danilo had come to America in the pre-democracy days, and he kept telling Ernest that it must now be better in Poland— more work, money, food. There was more, he couldn't really express it—more vodka, he could have a girlfriend, go into the city and party. His family couldn't call that often, but he would at least call one Sunday out of the month, and they told Danilo life on the farm was mostly the same. Danilo often told Ernest how he couldn't sleep, wondered if his leaving was a mistake. Ernest would tell Danilo worry invents a sore heart. Why not go take a break, he'd tell him. Then recognized his lie: All he seemed to do was live in a worrisome sea of memory and regret, his heart feeling soft and bruised, a shadow of purple inhabiting the edges of his hands. All he could do was take a seat on a stool, pick up a book, and begin reading. He'd look up occasionally to watch the packers fill another box, their hands striking along the glued seal as they closed it, and every hour he'd get up and check the running conditions of their extruders and write them down on his and Danilo's paperwork, while Danilo slept in the back storeroom. Ernest liked Danilo's quietness, for they seemed to bond with only a few words, their mutual silence a respite against any worry, and in the presence of a page, the purple shadow lightened into a July blue, his reading offering him some deeper current flowing faster than his shame.

Dave? What he doing? Danilo asked. Danilo turned to Ernest's hopper and beat against the bottom with a wrench, trying to sense how much material was left.

Ernest checked the gauges on the control panel, the extruder's amps holding steady. If the machine ran out of material, the extruder's die would begin to burn, and they'd need to shut the line down. While the die cooled and the hopper refilled, Ernest and Danilo would take apart the die and clean it up, gently rubbing away the burnt material without scratching the die, and then they'd need to put it all back together and start up the line again. A three-to-four-hour job—and Ernest knew someone would answer for the downtime, why the machine ran out of material.

Ernest reset the emergency lights. He flipped the manual material switch to try and drop the upper load of powder. The yellow hopper light flashed. Up above them, Dave beat on the lines. Ernest looked up, the bright lights covered in a filmy gauze, a golden dust of powder falling down. The floor hummed, steady and solid under his feet. Dave tripped on a hose, kicked up more dust and resin, and dropped the steel bar he held. Ernest pushed in his ear plugs a little tighter.

Danilo nudged Ernest in the ribs.

Cudva-Dave. *Hey*, don't worry, Danilo yelled, raising a flattened palm to Dave, then rubbing the top of his brow, wiping down his face and stroking his beard. Ernest and Danilo laughed.

Cudva. Ernest didn't know how to spell the word, and he never knew what it meant. Danilo used the word often. One day Ernest asked him to explain. It was a bad word, and even though Ernest never fully understood, he realized there was some Polish word—*cudva* or maybe *kudra*—that meant whore, or worse. The word endeared Danilo to him, the hard formality of its pronunciation, the same way Danilo was the only one to ever call him *Ernesto*. At the last Vulcan Christmas party, over at the Polish American Club, Danilo and Ernest had been the only ones left, dancing with two of the women who had served dinner. Ernest put five records on the turntable next to the Christmas tree, and in the open circle in front of the long tables and the torn pieces of wrapping paper, Danilo and the women showed him all the moves—the composition of an arm draped over a shoulder to a leg kicked out; hands moving with gestures that shifted their hips and feet as if they were puppets tied to long strings; the jiggle of breasts, the arc of waists, the curl of wet hair against the nape of a neck; the form and grace of four people circling in the balance and elegance of an alcohol- and laughter-induced choreography. Ernest, caught up in the vodka, the music, the warm sweat of their bodies, held Danilo around the neck and crooned, *Ay cudva-sito*. Danilo burst out with laughter, the women smiled and shook their heads, as if there were some form of confidence between these two wet, pink-faced men, who from such distant geographies could laugh and hold each other and create their own familiarity through the musical touch of flesh.

Dave beat at the hopper, a *Goddamn* coming down to Danilo and Ernest.

Ernest yelled back: Hold it, Dave. Just don't fuck with it for a minute. Ernest tried to restrain his temper. Sometimes these twelve hours, the loud machinery, his ear plugs clogging his mind, his feet sore from standing—Ernest couldn't help himself, could not stop his anger, which made his presence here even more solid, the cement under his feet hard and brutal. He only wanted Vulcan's to be a dream, a lonely garden where he was left alone to live within himself and wait for the next shift punching the time clock so he could then walk out into another, suddenly awakened life. Except for talking to Danilo, he wanted to be no one—only an anonymous man trying to earn a wage.

Dave put down the bar on the catwalk. He leaned on the railing.

What do you want to do? he yelled down.

Ernest retrieved his stool and set it under his hopper next to the extruder. Danilo stepped up onto the stool's seat, and Ernest handed him a wrench. If the hopper didn't drop material, its sensor might be caked. Danilo could strike the sensor's two prongs, knocking off the caked powder, and then it would sense its emptiness and drop the load. Danilo stepped from the stool to the extruder. He opened the hopper door. He didn't use the wrench, holding it in his left hand, and stuck his arm inside. He grimaced, reached deeper. The spinning yellow light went out. He pulled back, powder bursting from the door, onto the side of his turned face, his beard smudged with gold dust. He slammed the door shut, dropped the wrench to the ground, jumped down.

Ernest brushed the powder from Danilo's face with a rag. He looked up and gave Dave an OK.

When Dave stepped back, turning to move down the catwalk, he kicked the steel bar he had been using; it seemed to Ernest to leap off the catwalk—caught in golden dust, tumbling slowly, it floated for a moment as if buoyed by the dust. Ernest rushed forward and pushed Danilo out of the way, the steel bar striking the base of Ernest's neck. The sharp pain drove him to the floor. He lay on his side, his legs trembling. An ear plug fell out of his ear and rolled away into a pile of powder. He let his forehead fall, cool against the cement. He felt Danilo's hand on his shoulder.

Ay, coño. Coño, Danilo.

Danilo held the back of Ernest's head, rolled him gently onto his back.

Coño, a word Ernest gave to Danilo, a piece of his own language.

The weight of his head on the floor shot steely tremors down his spine. The floor rumbled and far in the distance he thought he heard a forklift honk. Ernest lay there, the moment too still, his sense of time and space clogged with inaudible sounds from the loudspeaker. He looked into Danilo's face as he held Ernest's arms still. They wouldn't stop shaking.

Don't move—go for help, Ernesto. Be back, Danilo told him.

Up above him, Ernest saw the smoke from the extruder coiled around blinking red and yellow lights. There were three loud pops like an extruder that ran out of material, the screw and die burning, yet this sound was even more tinny and bright: firecrackers—and then a rapid succession of louder pops ran together. A barrage of yelling followed, the smoke continuing to circle above him, and he felt a deep silence overtaking the plant. Just a moment ago he could feel the forklifts in his back and legs, their shifting and turning lifting through the concrete, but now the sensation—a rumbling, the striking of steel against steel— was gone. His eyes darted around, the pain in his spine too sharp to turn his neck, the high rafters filled with shafts of light and pools of gray and gold shadows, a sparrow suddenly gliding from the darkness through the smoky light. Blackness—the power cutting out for a moment—and then the lights surged back on, and Ernest sensed a heavy coldness following the quieting of the extruders, the saws no longer buzzing, the red and yellow lights now flashing without the hum of work.

Danilo's face was streaked with tears and blood. He raised his hands across his chest, his fingertips maroon, his arms wet. He dropped to his knees.

Okay, Ernest . . . *Crazy,* Danilo yelled, John crazy—he shooting everyone and then run out. He gasped for air, his shoulders shaking, and then he quickly turned and looked back as if someone were coming. Ernest tried to raise his hands to Danilo's arm, he could now see the gunshot wound in his shoulder, but he couldn't raise his hands off the floor. He wanted to say, *What?* He grit his teeth, and then he asked: How many?

Danilo wiped his face, his eyes, and pulled on his ears hard and long, the lobes throbbing white, red, white when he let go. He leaned on his elbow, shook for a moment, and then lay down next to Ernest, his boot touching Ernest's left ankle.

Six, seven . . . maybe ten, he said. In a whisper: Dave, think that *cudva* dead.

They lay there and although Ernest tried to focus on the beat of his breathing in his ears, he couldn't block out the yelling and wailing in the background, up near the time clock and the offices, and then he discovered he was focused on the sirens, praying that someone would soon arrive for Danilo.

When a stretcher was slid underneath Danilo, Ernest felt a strong rush of cold air, Danilo's hand leaving his shoulder. Ernest closed his eyes, waited for his own stretcher, felt in the cold a deep winter of snow and wind unfolding ahead of him, felt Danilo's arm around his waist as they glided across the dance floor, Ernest's mind filled with sweat and laughter as he danced away from the factory in a swirl.

For six months Ernest didn't work. In the first few weeks he took medications for the pain, lost his sense of taste, his arms shaky and weak, his eyes often blurring. Vertigo set in, and one day he fell on an icy sidewalk, causing greater pain. He quit taking the medications, and the doctor prescribed daily home therapy and sessions with a physical therapist twice a week. Each morning Ernest sat in front of the mirror on his bathroom door, a steel pulley hooked to the top, and suspended from the pulley was headgear and a twenty-pound water bag. It seemed to be the ultimate form of solitude; Ernest's hair sticking out of the headgear, the straps pressing into his cheeks, staring at his naked reflection, his mouth closed shut, his hands resting on his thighs, Ernest staring at a young man he didn't know: In these moments he began to wonder how much more he would endure to discover himself, to lose these canvas straps around his face, pulling on his neck muscles.

Gold stalks swaying in the dawn, an ox taking the rise of a red clay road, the bottom of a frayed burlap sack powdered with dust. Would his memory ever help him to discover something beyond a life of physical labor and pain?

He rubbed his knees, rubbed back across his thighs, up along his torso—but the pain drove his hands down. He couldn't lift his hands to his face, let alone his chest.

On Tuesdays and Thursdays, in the late afternoon, he would go to the physical therapist's office. The huge man—a former football player—laid Ernest down on a high table. He held his shoulders with the weight of his chest and an arm, and then twisted Ernest's neck, pulled on his head, trying to coerce Ernest's muscles away from atrophy. This was now the greatest source of discomfort; after he fell on the sidewalk, Ernest spent the first three weeks of December in bed, getting up only to go to the bathroom or the kitchen. A form of arthritis had been diagnosed from too much inactivity (and Ernest thought from perhaps reinjuring his neck when he fell on the ice). Sitting in certain chairs for too long, rolling out of bed quickly, his neck snapped, his shoulder and neck muscles locking up. He began to take long, hot showers, took to wearing a turtleneck and a scarf inside his apartment. Throughout his life, on a cold winter morning, Ernest's neck will remind him of his time in the factory. He'll see the bloom of blood on Danilo's shoulder, his sad lips, his beard streaked in pink. But for the next six months he luxuriated in the pain.

Moving outside his apartment, walking down that January's sidewalks and stepping onto a bus that swerved along the river, past the duck ponds and the river walk, Ernest stood in the aisle, waited, and got off in front of the college. Not having graduated from high school, he took a test to receive his GED. Then he was required to pass an introductory course in English before his other courses received credit. From January to the end of May he was driven by a desire to stay away from Vulcan's. The pain stayed, he continued to sit in front of the mirror in the morning and get therapy twice a week, and he continued to receive his workman's compensation checks and sit in classrooms.

Cognitive psychology. Composition. Petroglyph. Collage. Allegory and *metaphor, allegro, andante.* These words became a great opening into discovery and form, the rising tempo of some foreign future he was traveling toward. *Someone with fever / buried / in the darkness of a room. This is the tenor, this is the vehicle: outside I could see cool, blue shadow on a white wall.*

He sat in the back of the room, as far away from the others as he could, in the corner by the window. He looked up from his notebook, snow falling in thick white webs. He focused on the teacher writing on the chalkboard. His legs sprawled in front of him, his hand voraciously writing down everything the woman wrote and said, his eyes taking in her exact gesture, her hand on her hip, her finger around a piece of chalk she cut the air with to emphasize the rhythm of a phrase or the specific lighting within a scene, the way she always tucked her hair behind her ear, her lobe dusting with blue. His eyes strained, his ears anticipated. He lived to take notes and read books, as if his true fate had arisen, the dam in his heart suddenly bursting, Ernest swept into a fast and cold and clear creek.

His fingers felt the impressions of sounds and smells, his fingertips grazing each and every letter with excitement and awe.

Late at night, under a green lamp, with a scarf on, he stayed with his books for as long as his neck held his head up. Eventually it became lighter, his neck stronger, and his hands found a new sense of work on the solid plane of a wooden desk. One night he drew three oddly lined shapes on single sheets of yellow paper. They looked like flowers that had been pressed in between the pages of a book, a long stain he once saw on an uncovered mattress he had slept on in a shack in between picking corn and bagging potatoes, more natural and shapeless than the outline of a human body. He remembered the days he couldn't seem to move, his neck locked up, and Danilo would drop off a book he requested from the library. Every time, he was grateful to see him, Danilo rubbing his shoulder, smiling. Once, Danilo brought alongside the book a fifth of vodka. It wasn't quite noon but Ernest invited him in. He built a fire in the wood-burning stove, took out two short glasses, and placed a chunk of smoked whitefish and a wedge of cheddar cheese on a cutting board with two knives. They toasted the end of winter, ate and drank in silence, nodded with a kind of pleasure when the stove cracked with heat.

Every day, Ernesto, I cannot stop—I see them, Danilo said, his right hand massaging his left shoulder. He pulled on his beard, shot back his drink.

Ernest reached for the bottle, filled Danilo's glass, not sure what he could say, only knowing it was good to let Danilo say whatever he needed.

It is like small river, or the shores of a lake—very close to our machines, the blood. Danilo took a small sip. Don't know if I should go back.

Ernest looked at the drawings on the yellow sheets. In the outlines he saw shadows—ghostly, purple and blue, figures becoming distinct as they stepped from a row of corn, a line of lilac bushes, or stood on a riverbank in the dusk. He had lived across the border in a small town in Michigan, a region that betrayed the hearts of those he had somehow ignored. On a fourth piece of paper he drew what might look like a very crooked lake, and underneath he wrote *Danilo*. The crack of ice on the trees outside the library sounded clear as church bells on Sunday, the sound transformed into a feeling of comfort, pieces of ice thudding to the ground, and he focused hard on the bare limbs he could make out in the moonlight swaying in the wind, the cracking ice giving way to an open path he still needed to follow. There was something new, some change along that path. He had moved ten miles across the border, and here on the other side he seemed to live only with silence and memory. He slowly realized that only a handful of people cared for him, and now they were far away. Maybe the region had never betrayed them—or him. He had let them go, they had disappeared without a fight, and in that loss he needed to become more than he'd ever dreamed. He wondered what would happen to Danilo.

He scratched out his name.

He imagined within the two thick black lines cancelling it out, how the confusion and silence of his life held a mystery he never understood, let alone held and heard. He would have to learn to embrace that mystery—with *un abrazo fuerte*—so he could invent names for those figures standing in the dusk. Across those two black borders he might understand how to care for their hearts. Ice struck the window, Ernest lifted his head, followed the intimacy of a silver cloud crossing the moon.

The summer before, Ernest warmed his hands over a barrel. The broken railroad ties that he and Danilo had found on the side of the tracks glowed, the creosote crackling, small embers floating up and catching in the wind. Early June, an unseasonably stiff and cold wind sweeping down Western Avenue.

Danilo nudged him in the ribs. Ernest turned from the darkened road and brushed his hands close to the heat. Danilo handed him a cup of coffee and a donut.

They had laid their placards against the corner of the loading dock, now that it was turning dark. A group of strikers stood by the dock talking, drinking coffee and eating. The street was empty, wind and dirt dusting the curb at Ernest's and Danilo's feet. Joseph Maseros walked up from the dock.

Tell me again, Danilo. What did you say? Joseph asked, though not really speaking to Danilo. Instead, he looked at Ernest.

Danilo repeated that he didn't understand why they couldn't go back to work. *Cudva*-foremens, he said.

Ernest took a bite of his donut, sipped the edge off his coffee. He translated for Joseph that the foremen were always looking for reasons to question the way you did your job, trying to make more work for you. They made the twelve-hour shift feel like twenty-four. Ernest added, You know it makes you nervous, anxious. Sometimes I can't sleep knowing I have to come here.

Joseph rubbed his hands over the barrel, shrugged. He looked at Danilo and said: Everything they want for them. Tonight, this cold wind. The company works inside right now and do not sweat, and they think that they are right, that God gave them this cold.

Joseph shrugged again, squeezed Danilo's shoulder, and walked back to the dock.

Danilo patted Ernest on the arm.

Thank you. You know, right?

Ernest answered with a wink, the nod of his head. He put the rest of the donut in his mouth.

Out in front of them, deep inside the city of South Bend, a burst of white light. Kovaleski Stadium was coming to life for a baseball game.

Ah, see, Danilo pointed to the lights. One time I want to go— maybe me, you?

They had talked of going to watch a game, but many of the games were on nights they had to work. Ernest told Danilo that one day maybe they should go into Chicago and watch the Cubs play during the day.

What's next, Ernesto? It okay if you don't work, you go to school, no?

Ernest paused, his hands fisting with sweat.

I lose money too, Danilo. I want to work some more, before this place closes down for good.

Danilo dropped his paper cup into the barrel, opened both palms over the quick burst of flames.

Ernest often told Danilo that he would quit. And Ernest knew that Danilo could feel, most people felt it on the west side of town, that soon Vulcan's might close down, they would soon move their production south. From the turn of the century into the decade following World War II, South Bend was a vital center of production between Detroit and Chicago. Slowly, many plants closed, and when Vulcan's closed, South Bend would lose one of the last of the old employers, one of the last union plants. There was a palpable fear in the plant—and with that, rage.

There wasn't a car in sight. Behind them, out past the ethanol plant and across the fields, they could hear semis roaring over the bypass on the interstate. Earlier so many people passed and smiled and waved, yelled out encouragement to their brothers and fathers, their sisters and aunts, cousins and uncles. Some women from the P & A Club brought a box of donuts, some pans of baked chicken and noodles and sausage. Ernest listened to voices wailing out words that colored Western Avenue in a mosaic of languages. But no one spoke to him. For a moment he felt too self-conscious, unavoidably separate and apart from Danilo yelling back in Polish, waving his placard and his fist in the air. No one spoke to him. No one yelled out a language that was his own.

I go for a minute.

Okay. Ernest watched Danilo walk back to the dock. Joseph Maseros hugged Danilo around the head and pulled him under a circle of light. Joseph kissed him on top of the head. Danilo's brow glinted in the light, an imprint of saliva shining there. The men yelled and laughed. Danilo wiped his brow, and then all the men's voices rose up in a barrage of words foreign to Ernest.

He had never felt for certain what his role was among men like this. He felt disconnected from them but unsure whether he could ever fully cut himself away, cut the net that entangled him with men who worked hard all their lives, who died much too young. He saw his father—forced to quit school in the third grade—sweating, lifting a thick bundle of cane onto a cart pulled by a white ox.

The placards, the donuts and coffee, standing on the street, even in this moment, Ernest didn't know if he belonged. These men were fighting for a safe place to work, a decent wage, and a sense of pride for the time they put in to do a good week's work. Their contract had expired in May, and instead of negotiating for a small wage increase, an added paid holiday, and set limits on how fast a machine would run, the company insisted on changing every shift to a swing shift. If the company got their contract, every employee would be required to work four twelve-hour shifts a week, a form of mandatory overtime to force older workers to retire, to push production faster, and to eliminate fifty jobs. None of this would affect Ernest. He was young, had worked the swing shift of Tuesday/Wednesday and Saturday/Sunday from six at night until six in the morning for the last four years. He liked the swing shift, liked working with Danilo, and liked the extra money. He thought, too, that he could even use the time to attend classes and maybe create the chance to leave. To all the other men Vulcan's was their life, and for them to change, to meet killing production schedules, to give up the years and work they had given, and all work a swing shift—that was a fact that seemed distant, too hard, so outside of them they had to fight it.

Ernest finished his coffee. He looked into the barrel and dropped the cup inside. There was a burst of deep laughter. The men called Ernest. He turned back, Danilo standing under the loading dock light, a piece of chicken raised to his face.

Come over here, Ernest, the men yelled in unison, pointing at Danilo.

It never failed, no matter where he may be in the plant, down on his line, on break, ready to punch out, he'd hear his name over the loudspeaker. He'd go and find Danilo talking to a foreman or another worker, and they'd ask Ernest what Danilo was saying. At first he thought it a joke. But they called him more and more, and it became clear that people weren't listening. Although many of them were of Polish descent, English was their new mother tongue, and in between English and a few phrases in Polish, they did not seem to hear Danilo. For Ernest it was easy. In Danilo's voice Ernest heard his father calling him in the field, yelling for him in the middle of the night, telling him a story he had heard as a child. They spoke the same low, resonant English. *Beautiful* English, he thought.

Ernest walked forward and closed the space between them. Perhaps he could never actually leave these men. A year from now, his neck feeling stronger, he returns to work for three weeks in July. On his last day he walks down his line and stops at the puller and takes a hacksaw and cuts the panel in half. His line jams up, the air filled with smoke, the vinyl running out of the hot die onto the floor. Red emergency lights spinning rapidly, light arcing across the machinery, the cement floor. He walks up to the time clock and punches out for the last time, believing his gestures are credible, that he has cut himself away from this life.

The net returned one day as he drove down Western Avenue. He saw Danilo sitting against an abandoned building, his face turned up to the fall sun. Ernest pulled over, got out, and just as he was about to call out Danilo's name, he noticed his hands clasped across his stomach, almost black with dirt, his fingertips cracked with dried blood. He cleared his throat. Danilo slowly opened his left eye, squinted. He smiled, opened his other eye, and stood up.

Ernesto, Ernesto, ah, great to see you.

Hello, Danilo.

Danilo pulled out a pint of vodka from his jacket pocket and offered it to Ernest. He started to take it, and then stopped himself. There was a strong odor of urine between them, Danilo's hair no longer short but striking his collar, and it looked as if he hadn't washed it in some time. He held his hands tighter behind his back.

Maybe later—a little later I'll have a drink, Ernest said.

The front of Danilo's brown leather jacket was stained with yellow splotches, a tear beginning to break through the right knee of his jeans, and his left work boot was missing its lace, the tongue falling over the front of the toes.

What are you doing today? Ernest asked.

Ah, I came to buy, he shook the bottle, and squinted, shrugged his shoulders.

You going to Chicago, Danilo asked, and then started to laugh, but his throat gave way to a fit of coughing.

No, not Chicago. Spend the day with me, Danilo. I'm going to the lake.

Danilo took a quick drink, wiped his mouth with the back of his hand, shrugged again, nodded.

They got in Ernest's car and drove down Western Avenue. Ernest cracked the windows, turned west, and took Highway 31 to the north, the fields of dried corn golden in the afternoon light, the sky a bright blue, the highway empty and clear, making its way through the blazing fall-colored trees. There were two does grazing on the edge of a fence row, and when they passed a meadow with a small pond Ernest pointed as a thick-coated red fox stepped catlike on the muddy shore.

Ernest turned west off the highway just shy of St. Joe and followed a dirt road toward the lake. He pointed at the small cooler in the backseat. Danilo opened it and pulled out two beers. Ernest turned up the Mozart concerto playing on the radio, and they clinked the cans Danilo had opened, the beer icy cold and burning Ernest's throat. They could both easily see the creek winding through woods and around the edge of an apple orchard, the trees red and full with fruit.

Farmers Creek, Ernest said, and pulled in behind a line of pines that sheltered them from the road. Danilo got out, took a long drink, the can still wet in his hands. He let out a deep sigh, fought a burp, stepped back, and crushed the can under his boot. He threw it inside on the floorboard, closed the door, and walked up through the pines toward the creek.

Ernest opened the trunk. He pulled out his yellow rod, tested the knot on the silver-and-blue spoon, and decided he'd have Danilo use his rod. From a soft case he pulled out an old fly rod and put it together. He took up an older spinning reel he had recently put new line on, fitted it to the fly rod, guided the line through the eyes, and then tied up a snap swivel. He chose a lime green K. O. Wobbler and snapped it on. He had a small tackle box with spoons, swivels, some colored flies, and split shot weights to take along. He lifted his vest from the trunk, shrugged his arms through the holes, and slid the tackle box into the back pocket of the vest. He took a long drink of his beer, then left the can in the trunk.

When he cleared the pines he saw Danilo standing on the bridge holding a small pistol over his left arm, aiming down into the creek. Ernest heard the salmon plashing through the shallow rapids. Danilo fired. Then again. The sound from the shots lasted a few seconds, and then Ernest heard the salmon again, and in the distance the cawing of crows.

Danilo lowered the gun, and his arm shook violently. Ernest walked up, laid the two rods against the bridge, and looked down—flashes of green, silver, and red ribboning the creek— as the salmon knocked against each other making their way upstream.

The yellow one's for you, Danilo. He grabbed Danilo's arm and hand, held it until the shaking stopped. Danilo was crying.

Don't want to go back, Ernesto.

Ernest shook his head, turned to the creek and looked down, as if there were something there for Danilo to see in the running water. He felt quiet and at peace seeing the salmon make their way, red and gold leaves sliding by on the creek's surface. He let the sound of the water fill them, let it take shape in ways he could not control.

They were standing on the edge of a potato field, Ernest and his father, the arc of the irrigation sprinkler hitting his shoes, striking the plants' leaves with a cracking splash. When he stepped toward the shack, he tripped on a clump of thick weeds, the potatoes he carried in the upturned front of his T-shirt spilling to the ground. His father's eyes thinned and his jaw clenched, Ernest barely hearing *stúpido* as Changó brought his knuckles down on the top of Ernest's head. His skull suddenly tingled with sharp fire, he looked up past the tree branches into the blue bowl of sky, and remembered his abuela's palm following the shape of his head, how she sang a soft song of love and regret, and whenever an accident happened (spilling a cup of coffee, picking unripe mangoes, leaving the chicken coop door open), she would laugh from deep in her belly (*Ay, Ernestito*), and then pull him close.

Ernest grabbed the front of Danilo's shirt, pulled him close, pushed back, his closed fist striking Danilo's sternum with each pull and push, Danilo's arms swinging, the gun a trembling blue blur.

So easy, here, Ernest whispered and let go of his shirt. He raised his hand to the side of Danilo's face. *So easy.* He laughed, squeezed the back of Danilo's neck, *Take it easy, suave,* and pulled him close again. Ernest held him, felt Danilo release the gun, and he stepped back and tucked it into the side of his vest.

He looked deep into Danilo's wide gray eyes, the bottom rims watery in the cool air. A V of geese flew overhead, their honking suddenly overpowering the plashing of the salmon.

He told him, Danilo, so easy to cast our lines down there; out of instinct, out of anger, maybe being so tired before they die, one of them will grab the spoon. Ernest concentrated on his eyes, slowly opening and closing his hand so Danilo would consider their mouths, listen to his voice. He said, They don't eat anymore but still strike. It's easy to pull back, set the hook. Easier than shooting fish in a barrel. He was about to ask, *Have you heard that expression before,* but he knew in Danilo's laughter he had—or he realized how easy it had been to shoot the salmon. Danilo shook with laughter, held Ernest's shoulder for a moment. He pulled the bottle of vodka from his jacket and took a long drink. He wiped his lips, the top of the bottle, and handed it to Ernest.

Let's make hard, Ernesto.

Yes, why don't we do that—we'll make it harder for us.

Ernest handed Danilo the yellow fishing rod. Ernest closed his eyes and took a swallow, listened as the wind shook in the tops of the trees.

We'll walk down here about a mile or so to the mouth, down where the creek meets the lake—meets the *sea,* I say. Ernest slipped the bottle of vodka inside his pocket next to the gun.

It is open down there, and more room to fish? Danilo asked.

For sure. You can cast wide and far. Ernest pointed to the path that snaked along the creek through the trees, and then up high where the trees opened in blue. Danilo moved from the bridge and led the way. Ernest picked up his rod and followed behind, watching salmon gather and dart in the deeper stretches of the creek. There was a small logjam that gathered the creek into a pool, and Ernest pulled the gun from his pocket and tossed it into the pool, the splash of the gun sounding no different than the salmon rising over the logjam. If Danilo asked for it, he'd apologize for losing it, and promise to buy him another.

He broke stride and caught up to Danilo, who stopped for a moment, unzipped his jacket, took it off, and draped it over the crook of his elbow. The back of Danilo's denim shirt was lined with sweat. Ernest could see there were still two good hours of light. He imagined how surprised Danilo would be when he hooked into a steelhead, the yellow rod bent in a stiff arc, the green line taut with the trout taking out line and running toward deeper water. Danilo's palms turning warm and full with the thrumming pull of the rod—creek and sky and sea alive in his hands—and then Ernest's legs seemed to dance without him, taking giant steps, as he reached out and held Danilo's elbow, just when it seemed Danilo was about to slip on the path.

ACKNOWLEDGMENTS

The following appeared in various print and online journals in slightly different forms: "First Love" appeared in *Platte Valley Review;* "A Case of Consolation" in *Freight Stories;* "Someday You'll See" in *Grasslands Review;* "Acceptance" in *Quercus Review;* "Exile's Home" in *Pinyon;* "In the Fields of Memory" in *Crab Orchard Review: A Journal of Creative Works;* "Avenue of the Americas, circa 1952" (as "Black Shadow, circa 1952") and "Fallen Leaves, yellow, orange, green" in *Palabra: A Magazine of Chicano & Latino Literary Art;* "Waves" in *REAL: Regarding Arts & Letters;* and "Arrival, circa 1976, *El Morro*" and "The Shadows of Palms" in *Washington Square (2nd International Issue)*. The author thanks the editors of these journals for their support.

A few lines on page 99 are from Michael Ondaatje's *Handwriting* and Jean Rhys's *Wide Sargasso Sea*. The brief passage of remembered reading on page 87 is from A. A. Milne's *Winnie-the-Pooh*.

For over a decade Patricia Henley and Pablo Medina have been unwavering in their friendship and support. A note, a letter, a brief meeting can stay with me for months and is there in "the blush of the lamp, in the purity of white pages."

During the writing of this book, Francisco Aragón, Charles Fort, and Amy Hassinger have gifted their conversation and friendship.

Rob Davidson and Devin Johnston have become my *lectors* over the years. Although we are miles apart, you both honor what William Carlos Williams considered the particularity of poetry, "each speech having its own character." You nudge me toward accepting and celebrating my "talents and the will that drives them" toward beauty.

From the beginning, Kristen Buckles has been enthusiastically supportive of this book. I appreciate your listening to these "blues," Kristen, hearing the timbre of these characters, their lives, stories, and memories, and I thank you for helping them become residents in the imaginations and hearts of readers.

ABOUT THE AUTHOR

Fred Arroyo is the author of the novel *The Region of Lost Names* (University of Arizona Press, 2008). Named one of the Top Ten New Latino Authors to Watch (and Read) in 2009 by LatinoStories.com, Fred is a recipient of an Individual Artist Grant from the Indiana Arts Commission. Currently, he is working on a book of essays in which he lyrically meditates on work, reading and writing, migration and place. He is also writing a novel set primarily in the Caribbean. Fred lives in Southern California and teaches Chican@ and Latin@ literature and fiction writing at Whittier College. He is also a faculty mentor in the University of Nebraska MFA in Writing low-residency program.